Sir Arthur Conan Doyle's
The **Adventure** of the **Priory School**

Adapted by: Vincent Goodwin

Illustrated by: Ben Dunn

visit us at
www.abdopublishing.com

Published by Magic Wagon, a division of the ABDO Group, PO Box 398166, Minneapolis, Minnesota, 55439.

Printed in the United States of America, North Mankato, Minnesota.
042013
092013
This book contains at least 10% recycled materials.

Written by Sir Arthur Conan Doyle
Adapted by Vincent Goodwin
Illustrated by Ben Dunn
Colored by Robby Bevard
Lettered by Doug Dlin
Edited by Stephanie Hedlund and Rochelle Baltzer
Interior layout by Antarctic Press
Cover art by Ben Dunn
Cover design by Abbey Fitzgerald

Library of Congress Cataloging-in-Publication Data

Goodwin, Vincent.
Sir Arthur Conan Doyle's The adventure of the Priory School / adapted by Vincent Goodwin ; illustrated by Ben Dunn.
p. cm. -- (The graphic novel adventures of Sherlock Holmes)
Summary: Retold in graphic novel form, Sherlock Holmes is called in to investigate when the Duke of Holdernesse's only son disappears from the Priory School.
ISBN 978-1-61641-973-8
1. Doyle, Arthur Conan, Sir, 1859-1930. Adventure of the Priory School--Adaptations.
2. Holmes, Sherlock (Fictitious character)--Comic books, strips, etc. 3. Holmes, Sherlock (Fictitious character)--Juvenile fiction. 4. Graphic novels. [1. Graphic novels. 2. Doyle, Arthur Conan, Sir, 1859-1930. Adventure of the Priory School--Adaptations. 3. Mystery and detective stories.] I. Dunn, Ben, ill. II. Doyle, Arthur Conan, Sir, 1859-1930. Adventure of the Priory School. III. Title. IV. Title: Adventure of the Priory School.
PZ7.7.G66Sip 2013
741.5'973--dc23

2013003892

Table of Contents

Cast

Sherlock Holmes

Dr. John Watson

Dr. Thorneycroft Huxtable

Duke of Holdernesse

Arthur

James Wilder

Mr. Heidegger

Security Guard

Mr. Hayes

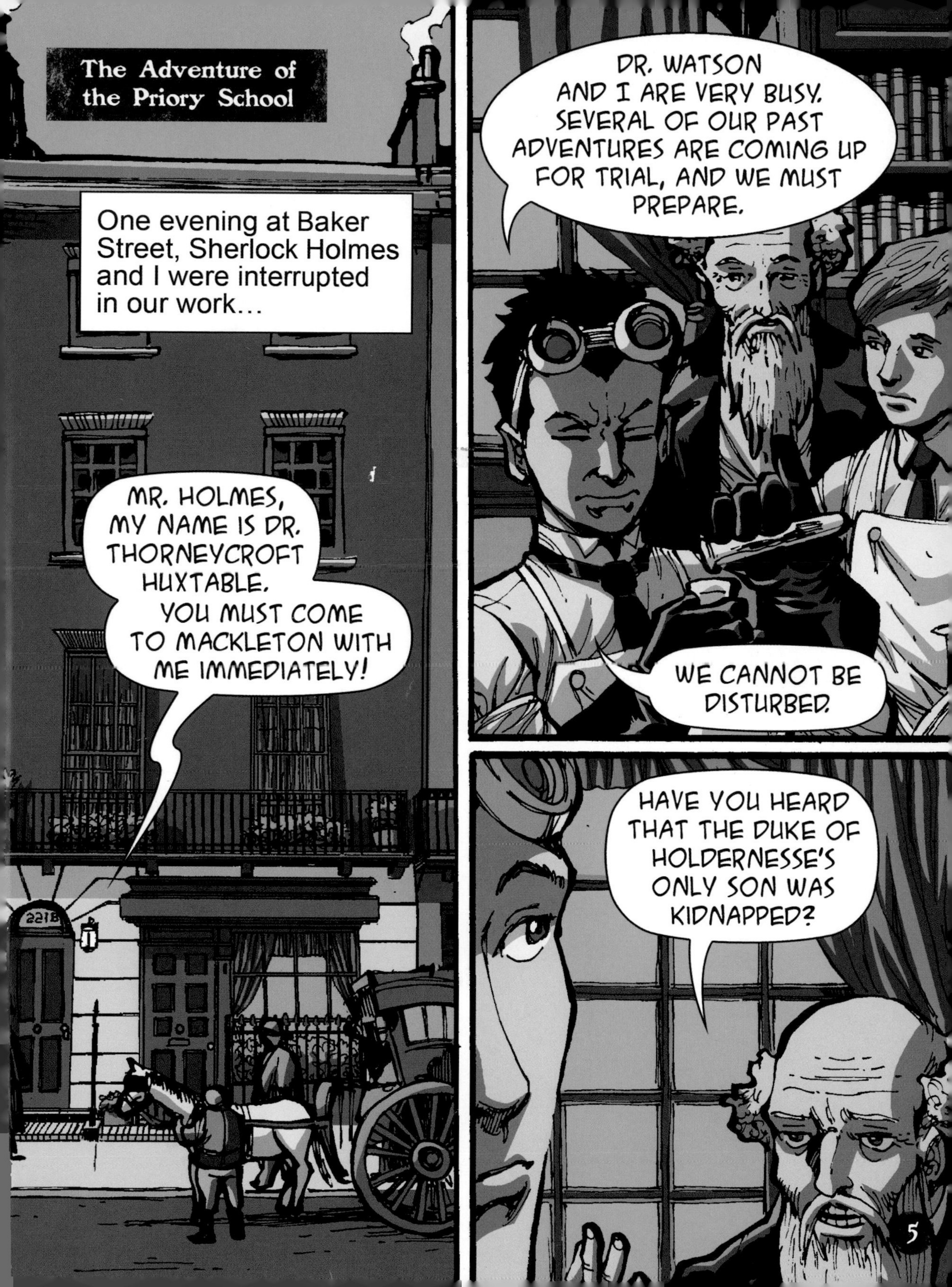

The Adventure of the Priory School
One evening at Baker Street, Sherlock Holmes and I were interrupted in our work…
MR. HOLMES, MY NAME IS DR. THORNEYCROFT HUXTABLE.
YOU MUST COME TO MACKLETON WITH ME IMMEDIATELY!
221B
DR. WATSON AND I ARE VERY BUSY. SEVERAL OF OUR PAST ADVENTURES ARE COMING UP FOR TRIAL, AND WE MUST PREPARE.
WE CANNOT BE DISTURBED.
HAVE YOU HEARD THAT THE DUKE OF HOLDERNESSE'S ONLY SON WAS KIDNAPPED?

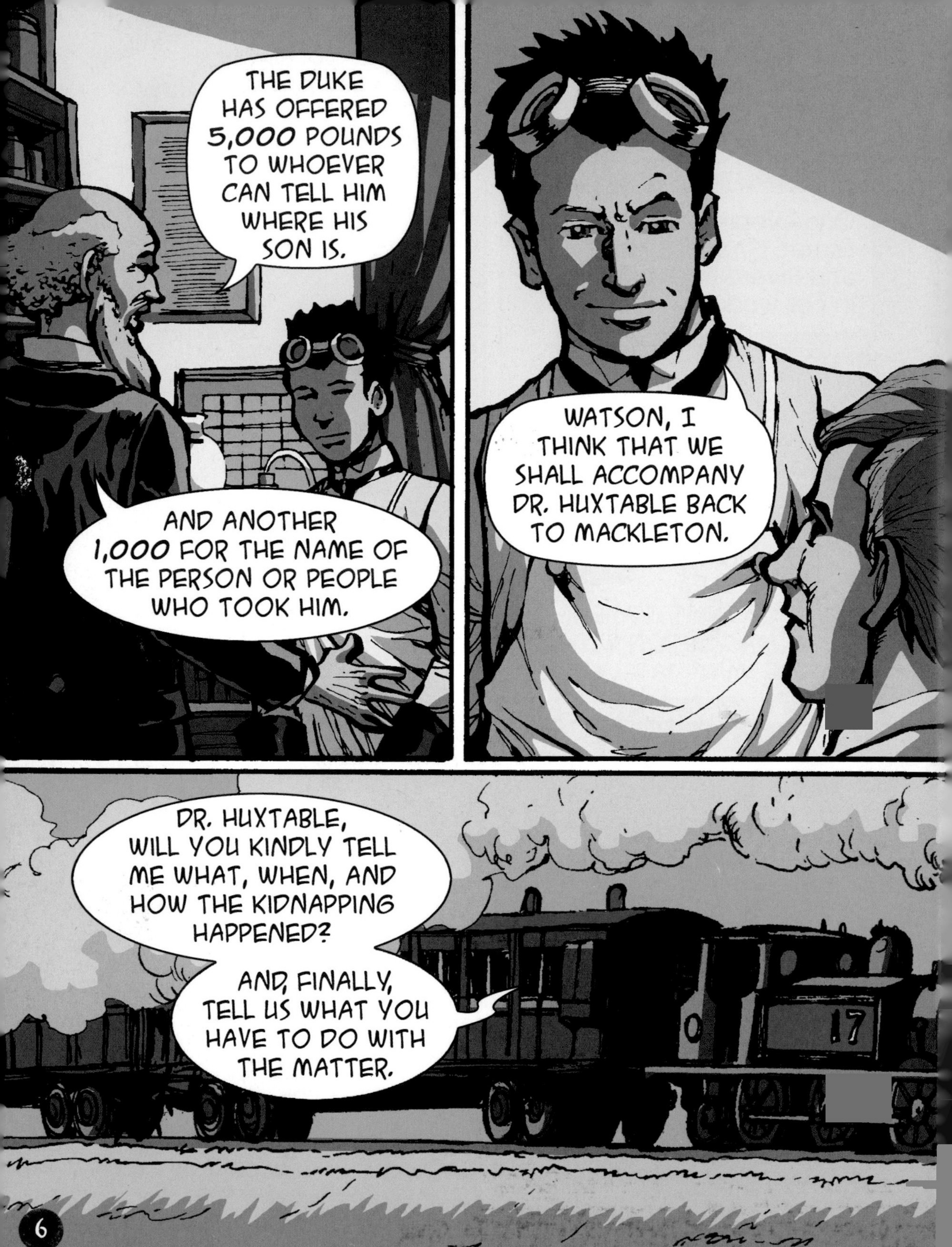
THE DUKE HAS OFFERED 5,000 POUNDS TO WHOEVER CAN TELL HIM WHERE HIS SON IS.
AND ANOTHER 1,000 FOR THE NAME OF THE PERSON OR PEOPLE WHO TOOK HIM.
WATSON, I THINK THAT WE SHALL ACCOMPANY DR. HUXTABLE BACK TO MACKLETON.
DR. HUXTABLE, WILL YOU KINDLY TELL ME WHAT, WHEN, AND HOW THE KIDNAPPING HAPPENED?
AND, FINALLY, TELL US WHAT YOU HAVE TO DO WITH THE MATTER.
17

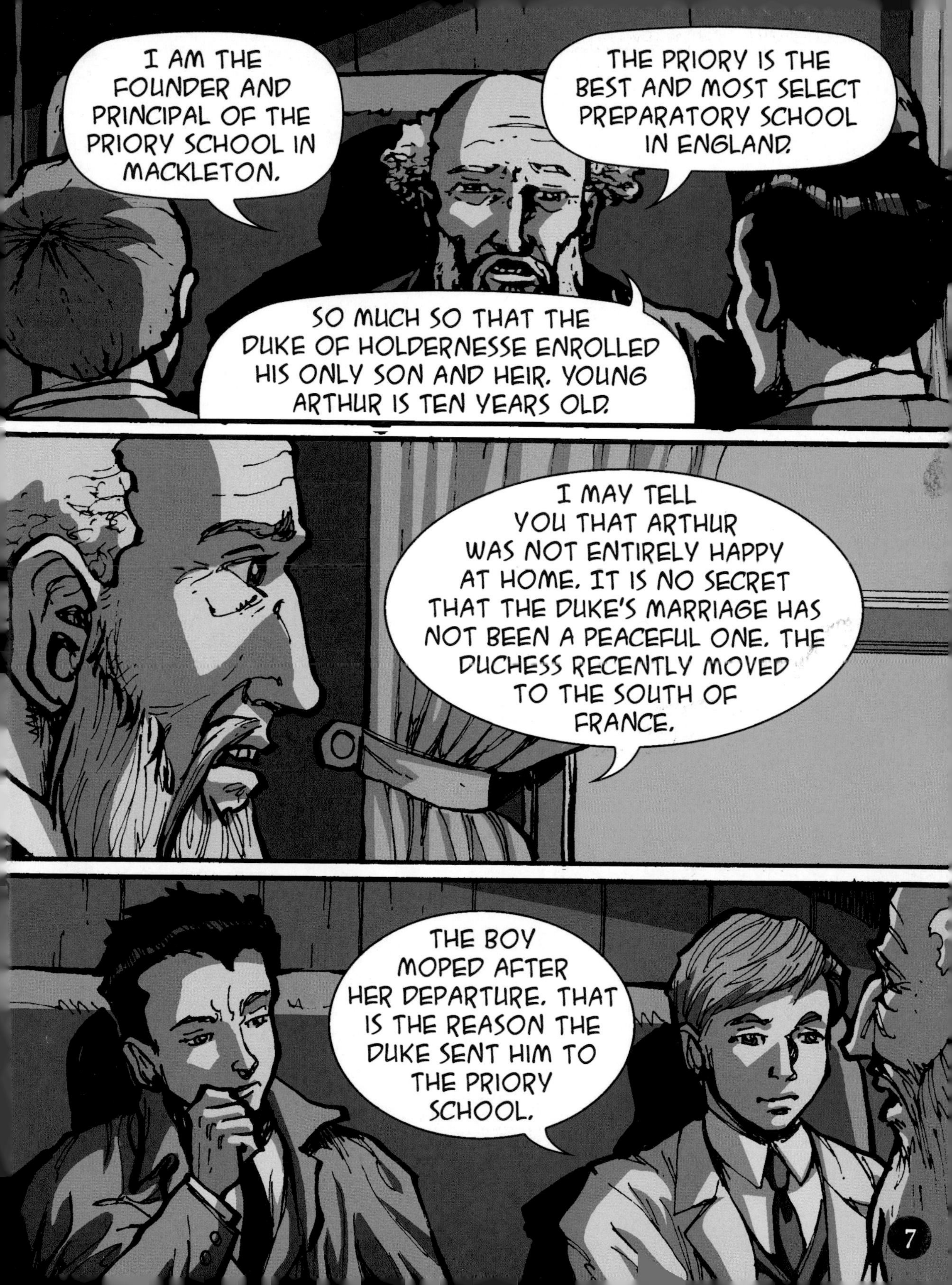
I AM THE FOUNDER AND PRINCIPAL OF THE PRIORY SCHOOL IN MACKLETON.
THE PRIORY IS THE BEST AND MOST SELECT PREPARATORY SCHOOL IN ENGLAND.
SO MUCH SO THAT THE DUKE OF HOLDERNESSE ENROLLED HIS ONLY SON AND HEIR. YOUNG ARTHUR IS TEN YEARS OLD.
I MAY TELL YOU THAT ARTHUR WAS NOT ENTIRELY HAPPY AT HOME. IT IS NO SECRET THAT THE DUKE'S MARRIAGE HAS NOT BEEN A PEACEFUL ONE. THE DUCHESS RECENTLY MOVED TO THE SOUTH OF FRANCE.
THE BOY MOPED AFTER HER DEPARTURE. THAT IS THE REASON THE DUKE SENT HIM TO THE PRIORY SCHOOL.

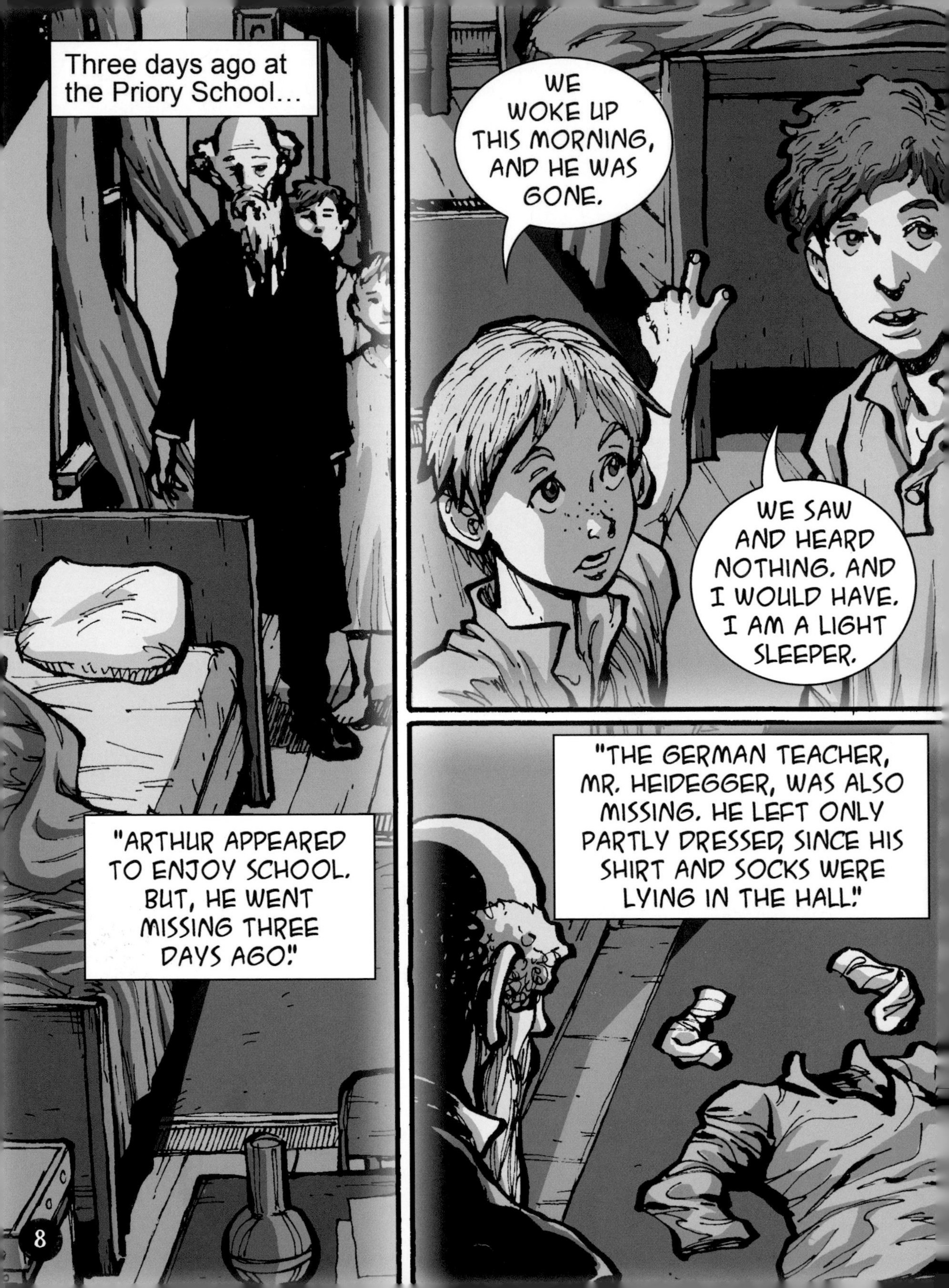
Three days ago at the Priory School…
"ARTHUR APPEARED TO ENJOY SCHOOL. BUT, HE WENT MISSING THREE DAYS AGO."
WE WOKE UP THIS MORNING, AND HE WAS GONE.
WE SAW AND HEARD NOTHING. AND I WOULD HAVE. I AM A LIGHT SLEEPER.
"THE GERMAN TEACHER, MR. HEIDEGGER, WAS ALSO MISSING. HE LEFT ONLY PARTLY DRESSED, SINCE HIS SHIRT AND SOCKS WERE LYING IN THE HALL."

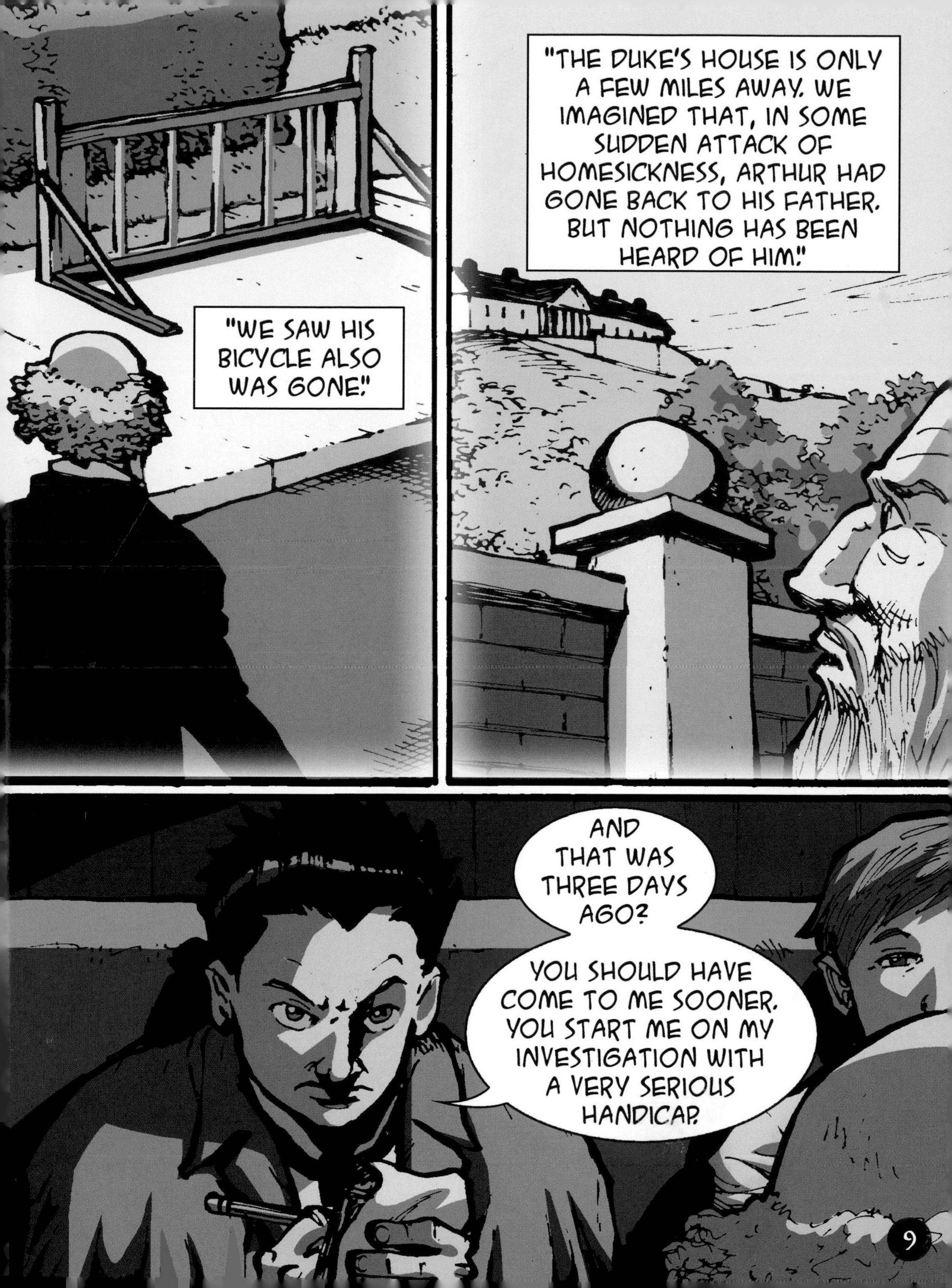
"WE SAW HIS BICYCLE ALSO WAS GONE."
"THE DUKE'S HOUSE IS ONLY A FEW MILES AWAY. WE IMAGINED THAT, IN SOME SUDDEN ATTACK OF HOMESICKNESS, ARTHUR HAD GONE BACK TO HIS FATHER. BUT NOTHING HAS BEEN HEARD OF HIM."
AND THAT WAS THREE DAYS AGO?
YOU SHOULD HAVE COME TO ME SOONER. YOU START ME ON MY INVESTIGATION WITH A VERY SERIOUS HANDICAP.

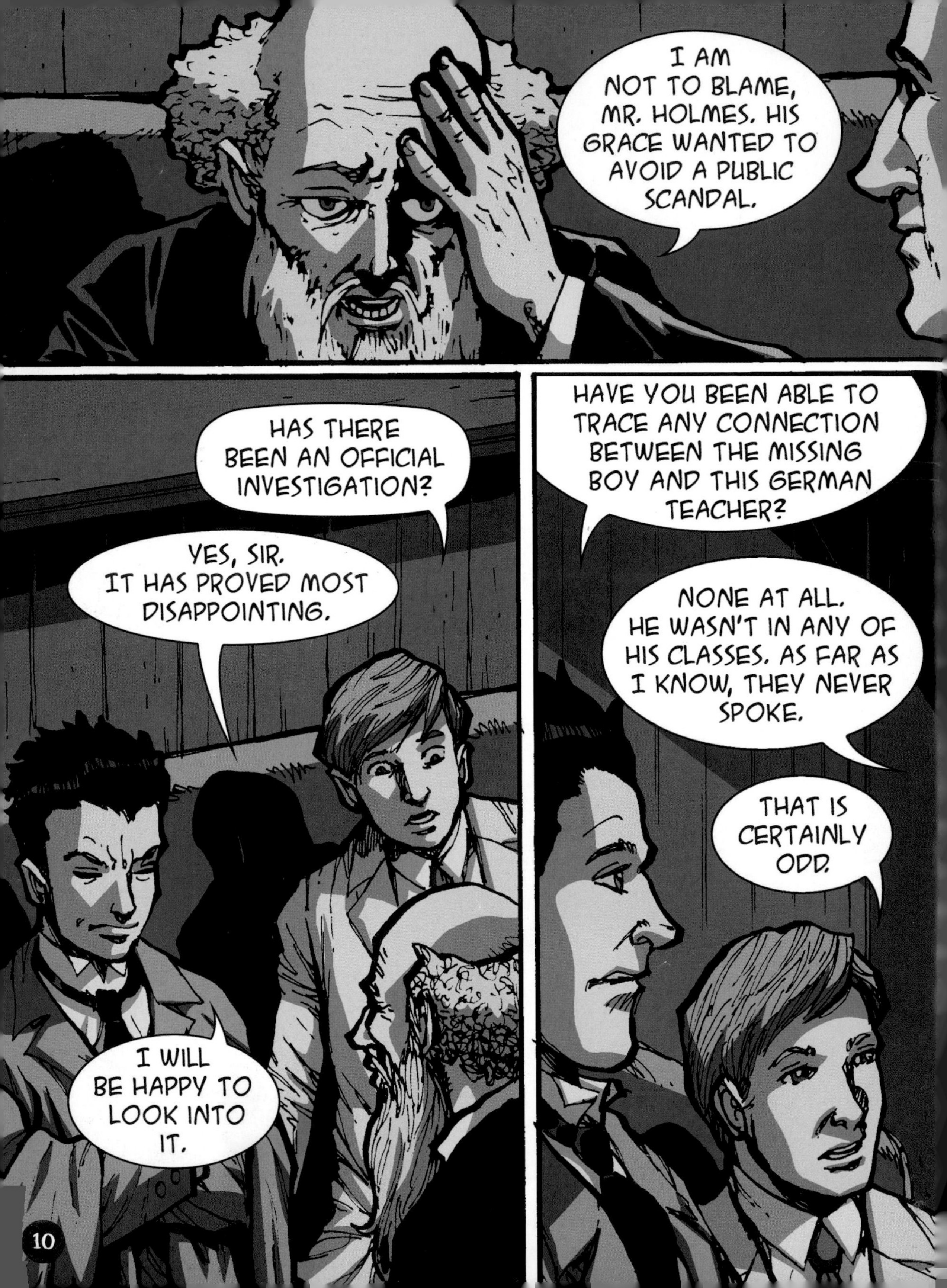
I AM NOT TO BLAME, MR. HOLMES. HIS GRACE WANTED TO AVOID A PUBLIC SCANDAL.
HAS THERE BEEN AN OFFICIAL INVESTIGATION?
YES, SIR. IT HAS PROVED MOST DISAPPOINTING.
I WILL BE HAPPY TO LOOK INTO IT.
HAVE YOU BEEN ABLE TO TRACE ANY CONNECTION BETWEEN THE MISSING BOY AND THIS GERMAN TEACHER?
NONE AT ALL. HE WASN'T IN ANY OF HIS CLASSES. AS FAR AS I KNOW, THEY NEVER SPOKE.
THAT IS CERTAINLY ODD.

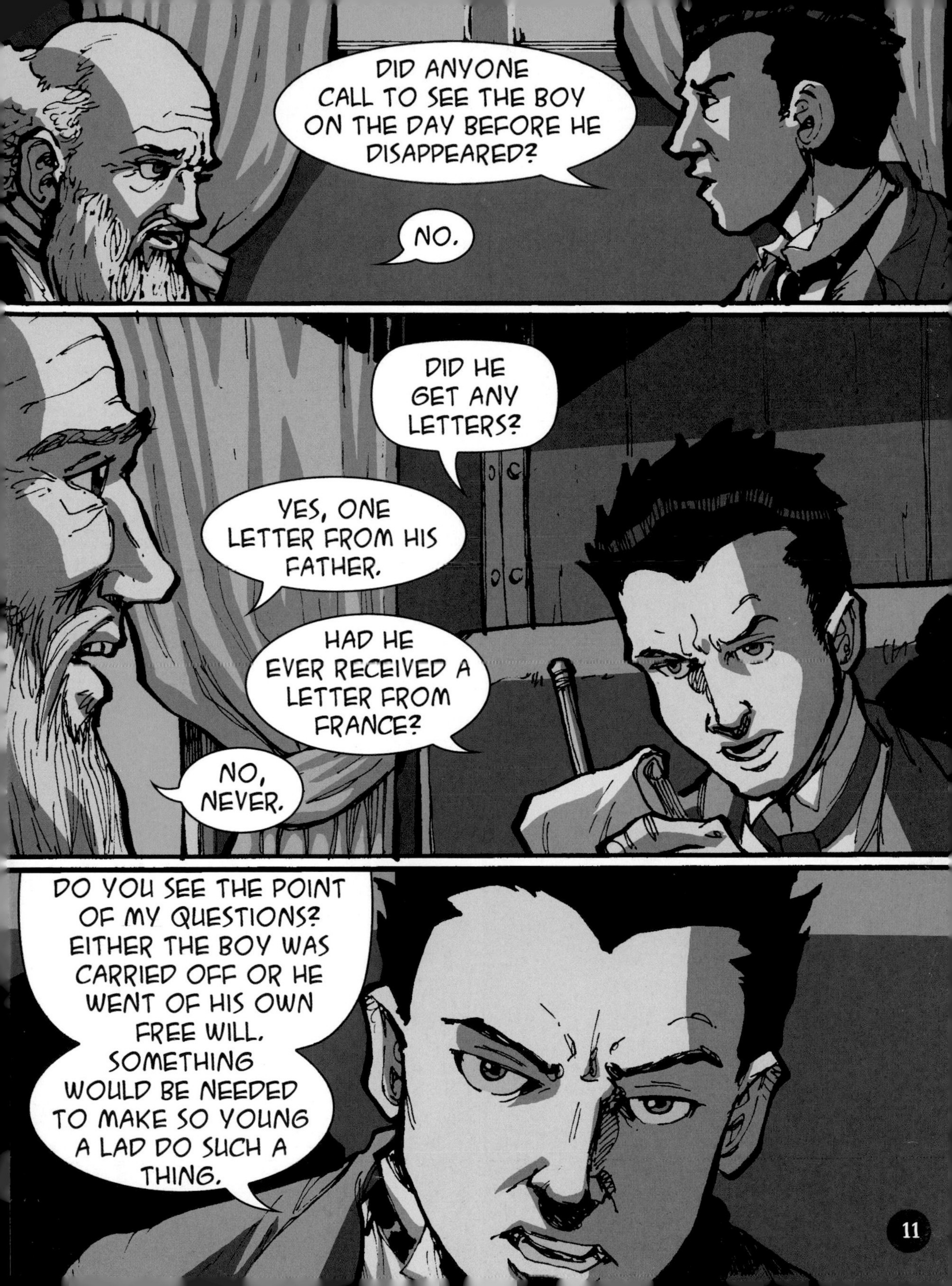
DID ANYONE CALL TO SEE THE BOY ON THE DAY BEFORE HE DISAPPEARED?
NO.
DID HE GET ANY LETTERS?
YES, ONE LETTER FROM HIS FATHER.
HAD HE EVER RECEIVED A LETTER FROM FRANCE?
NO, NEVER.
DO YOU SEE THE POINT OF MY QUESTIONS? EITHER THE BOY WAS CARRIED OFF OR HE WENT OF HIS OWN FREE WILL. SOMETHING WOULD BE NEEDED TO MAKE SO YOUNG A LAD DO SUCH A THING.

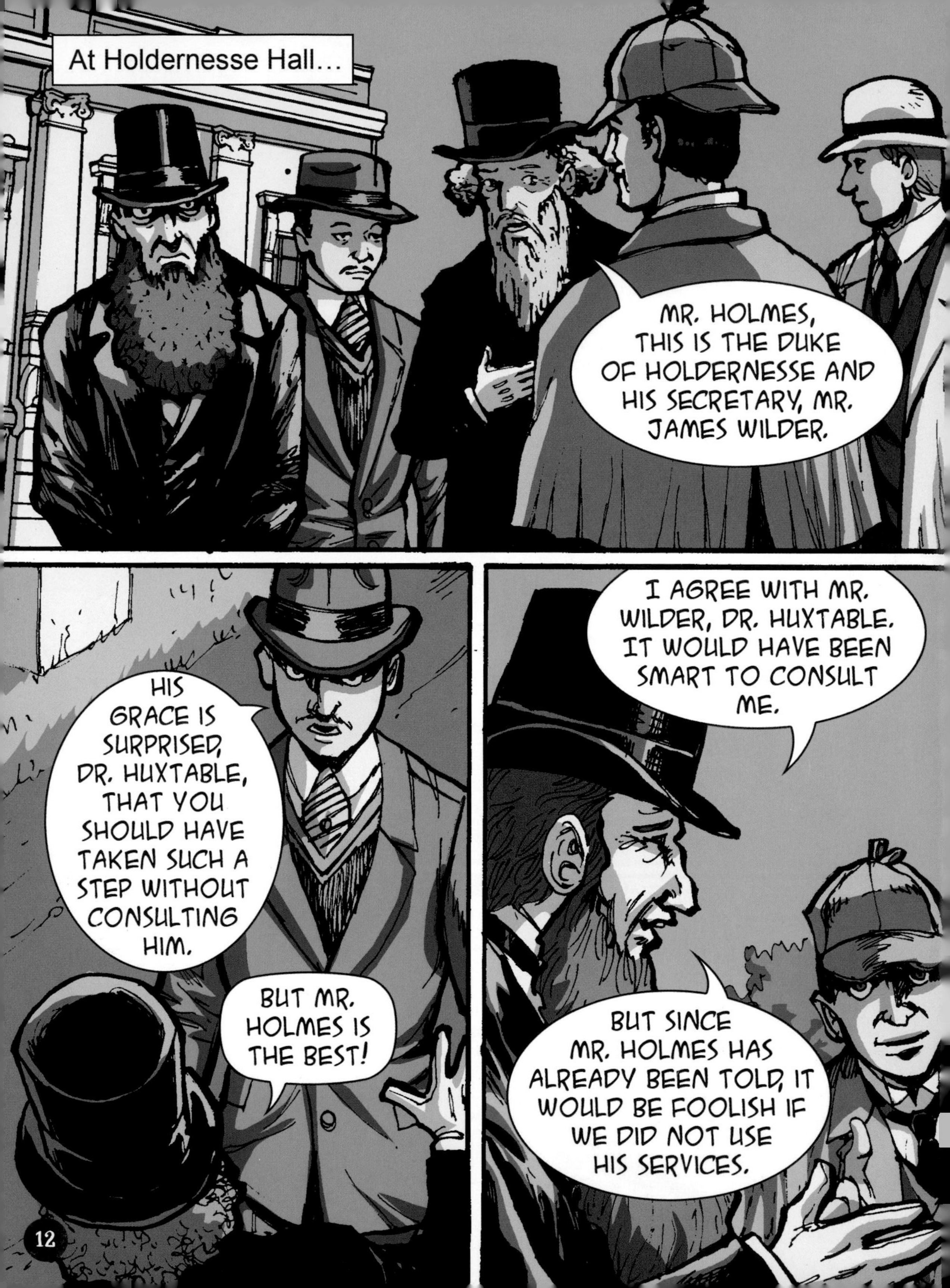
At Holdernesse Hall…
MR. HOLMES, THIS IS THE DUKE OF HOLDERNESSE AND HIS SECRETARY, MR. JAMES WILDER.
HIS GRACE IS SURPRISED, DR. HUXTABLE, THAT YOU SHOULD HAVE TAKEN SUCH A STEP WITHOUT CONSULTING HIM.
BUT MR. HOLMES IS THE BEST!
I AGREE WITH MR. WILDER, DR. HUXTABLE. IT WOULD HAVE BEEN SMART TO CONSULT ME.
BUT SINCE MR. HOLMES HAS ALREADY BEEN TOLD, IT WOULD BE FOOLISH IF WE DID NOT USE HIS SERVICES.

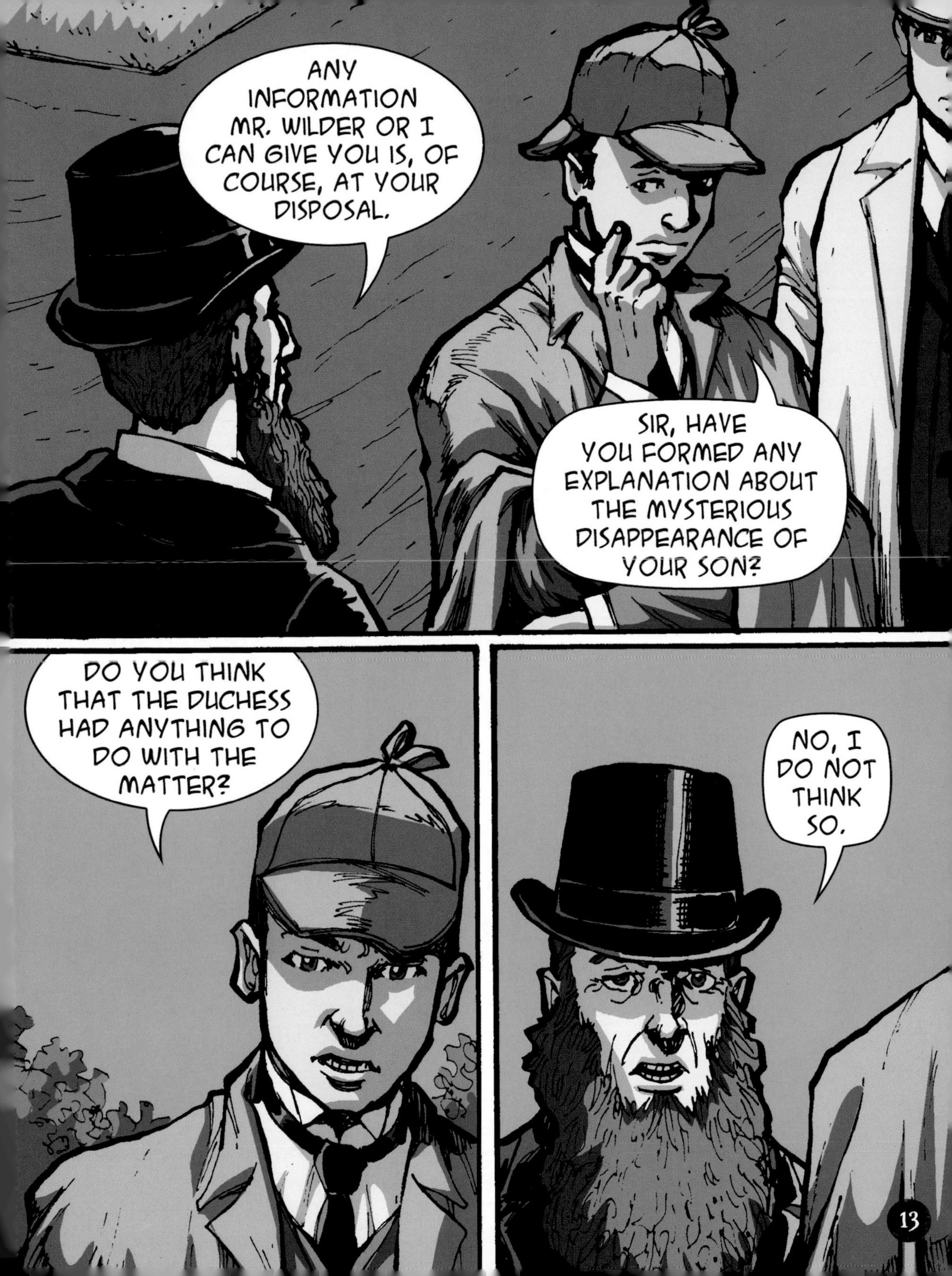
ANY INFORMATION MR. WILDER OR I CAN GIVE YOU IS, OF COURSE, AT YOUR DISPOSAL.
SIR, HAVE YOU FORMED ANY EXPLANATION ABOUT THE MYSTERIOUS DISAPPEARANCE OF YOUR SON?
DO YOU THINK THAT THE DUCHESS HAD ANYTHING TO DO WITH THE MATTER?
NO, I DO NOT THINK SO.

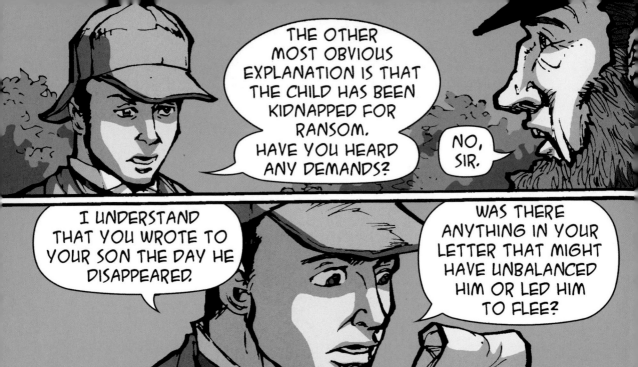

THE OTHER MOST OBVIOUS EXPLANATION IS THAT THE CHILD HAS BEEN KIDNAPPED FOR RANSOM. HAVE YOU HEARD ANY DEMANDS?

NO, SIR.

I UNDERSTAND THAT YOU WROTE TO YOUR SON THE DAY HE DISAPPEARED.

WAS THERE ANYTHING IN YOUR LETTER THAT MIGHT HAVE UNBALANCED HIM OR LED HIM TO FLEE?

THE DUKE HAS ALREADY SAID THAT HE DOES NOT BELIEVE THAT THE DUCHESS WOULD ENCOURAGE SO MONSTROUS AN ACTION. BUT THE LAD HAD THE MOST WRONGHEADED OPINIONS.

IT IS POSSIBLE THAT HE MAY HAVE FLED TO HER, AIDED BY HIS GERMAN TEACHER.

PLEASE FIND MY SON, MR. HOLMES. I WILL REWARD YOU HANDSOMELY.

THERE IS NOTHING HERE, EXCEPT THAT HE OBVIOUSLY ESCAPED THROUGH THE WINDOW.

I WAS AT MY POST FROM MIDNIGHT TO SIX. THIS IS THE ONLY ROAD, AND THERE'S NO WAY THEY COULD HAVE GONE BY WITHOUT ME SEEING.

"THEY DID NOT GO EAST."

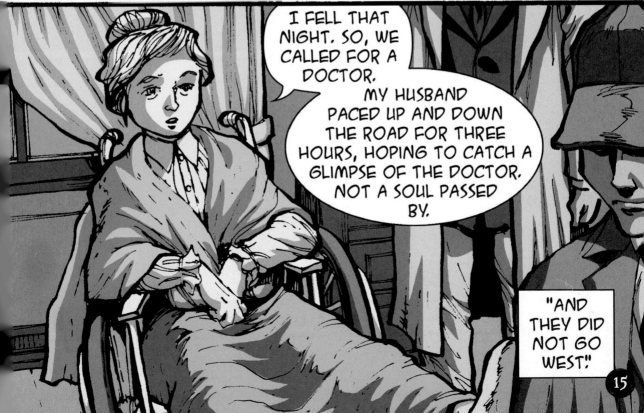

I FELL THAT NIGHT. SO, WE CALLED FOR A DOCTOR.
MY HUSBAND PACED UP AND DOWN THE ROAD FOR THREE HOURS, HOPING TO CATCH A GLIMPSE OF THE DOCTOR. NOT A SOUL PASSED BY.

"AND THEY DID NOT GO WEST."

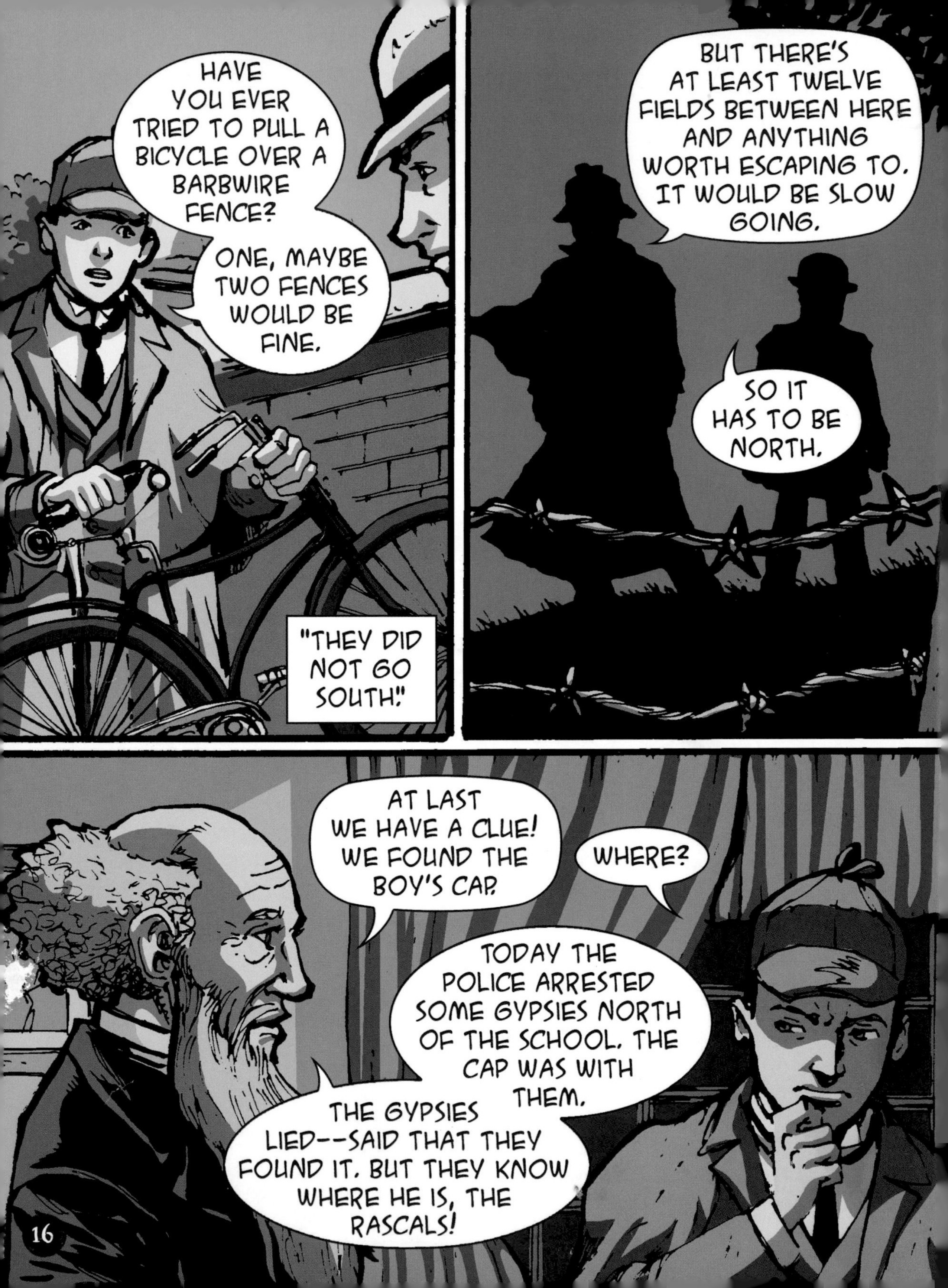
HAVE YOU EVER TRIED TO PULL A BICYCLE OVER A BARBWIRE FENCE?
ONE, MAYBE TWO FENCES WOULD BE FINE.
"THEY DID NOT GO SOUTH!"
BUT THERE'S AT LEAST TWELVE FIELDS BETWEEN HERE AND ANYTHING WORTH ESCAPING TO. IT WOULD BE SLOW GOING.
SO IT HAS TO BE NORTH.
AT LAST WE HAVE A CLUE! WE FOUND THE BOY'S CAP.
WHERE?
TODAY THE POLICE ARRESTED SOME GYPSIES NORTH OF THE SCHOOL. THE CAP WAS WITH THEM.
THE GYPSIES LIED--SAID THAT THEY FOUND IT. BUT THEY KNOW WHERE HE IS, THE RASCALS!

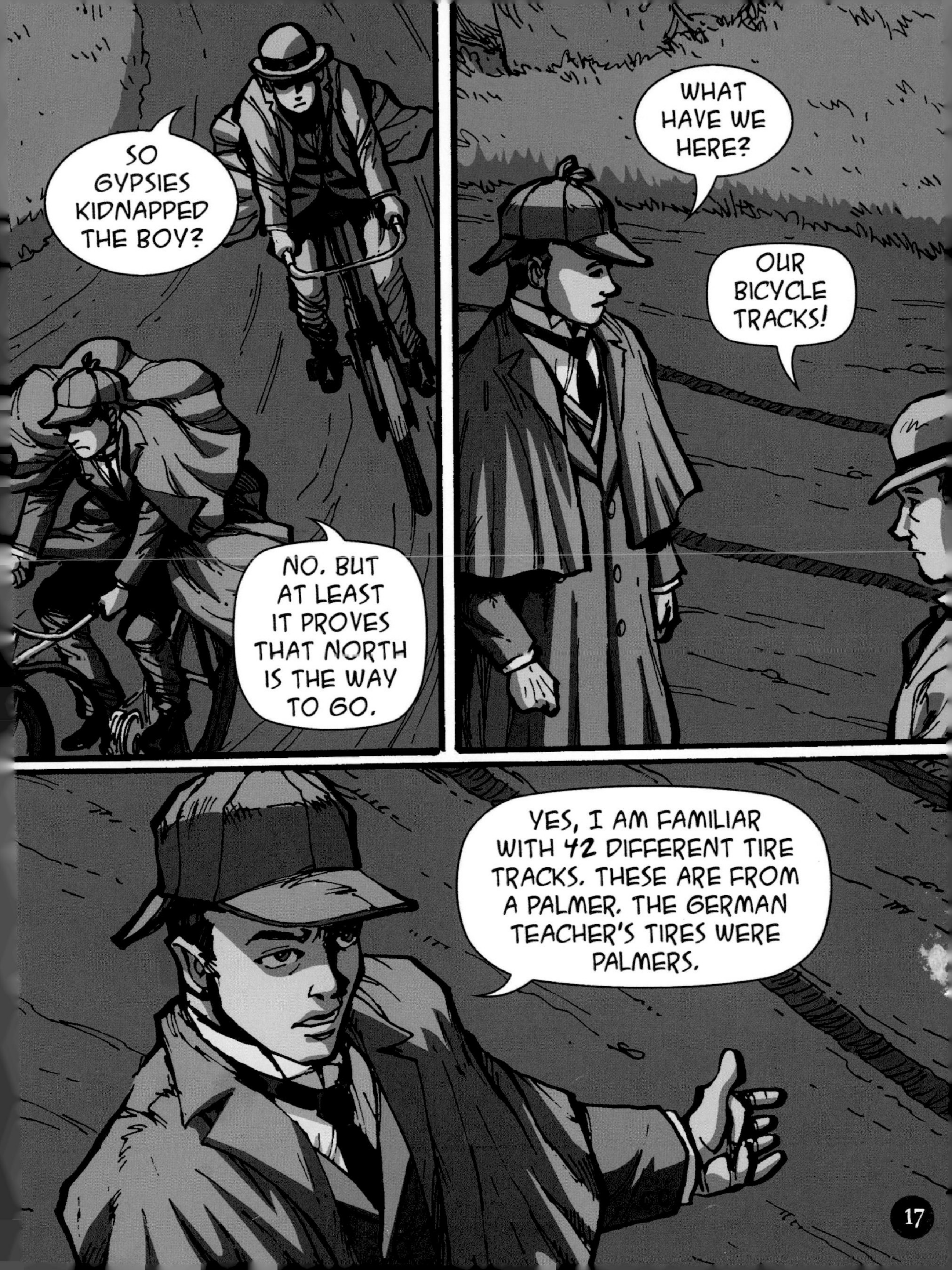
SO GYPSIES KIDNAPPED THE BOY?
NO. BUT AT LEAST IT PROVES THAT NORTH IS THE WAY TO GO.
WHAT HAVE WE HERE?
OUR BICYCLE TRACKS!
YES, I AM FAMILIAR WITH 42 DIFFERENT TIRE TRACKS. THESE ARE FROM A PALMER. THE GERMAN TEACHER'S TIRES WERE PALMERS.

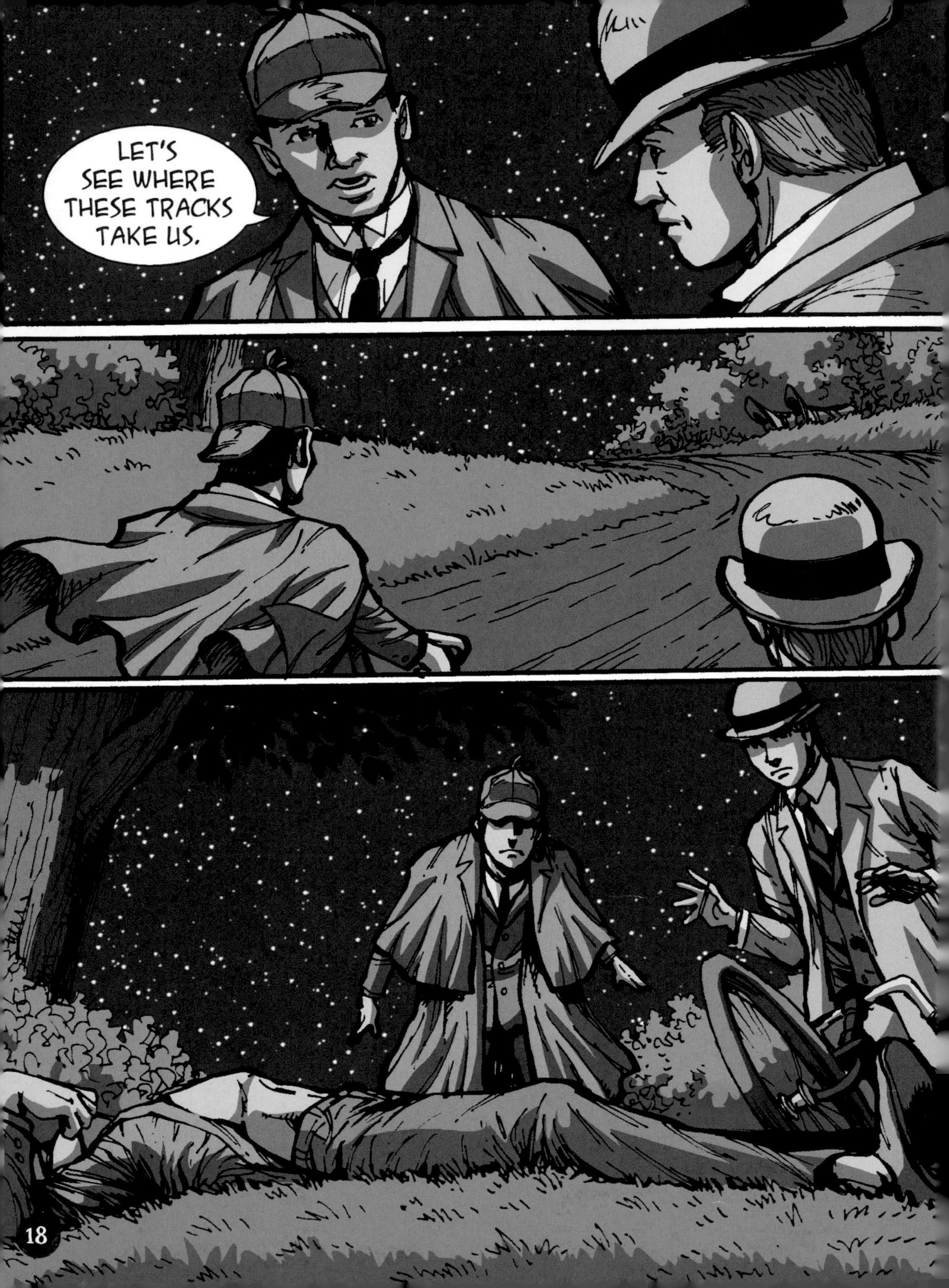
LET'S SEE WHERE THESE TRACKS TAKE US.

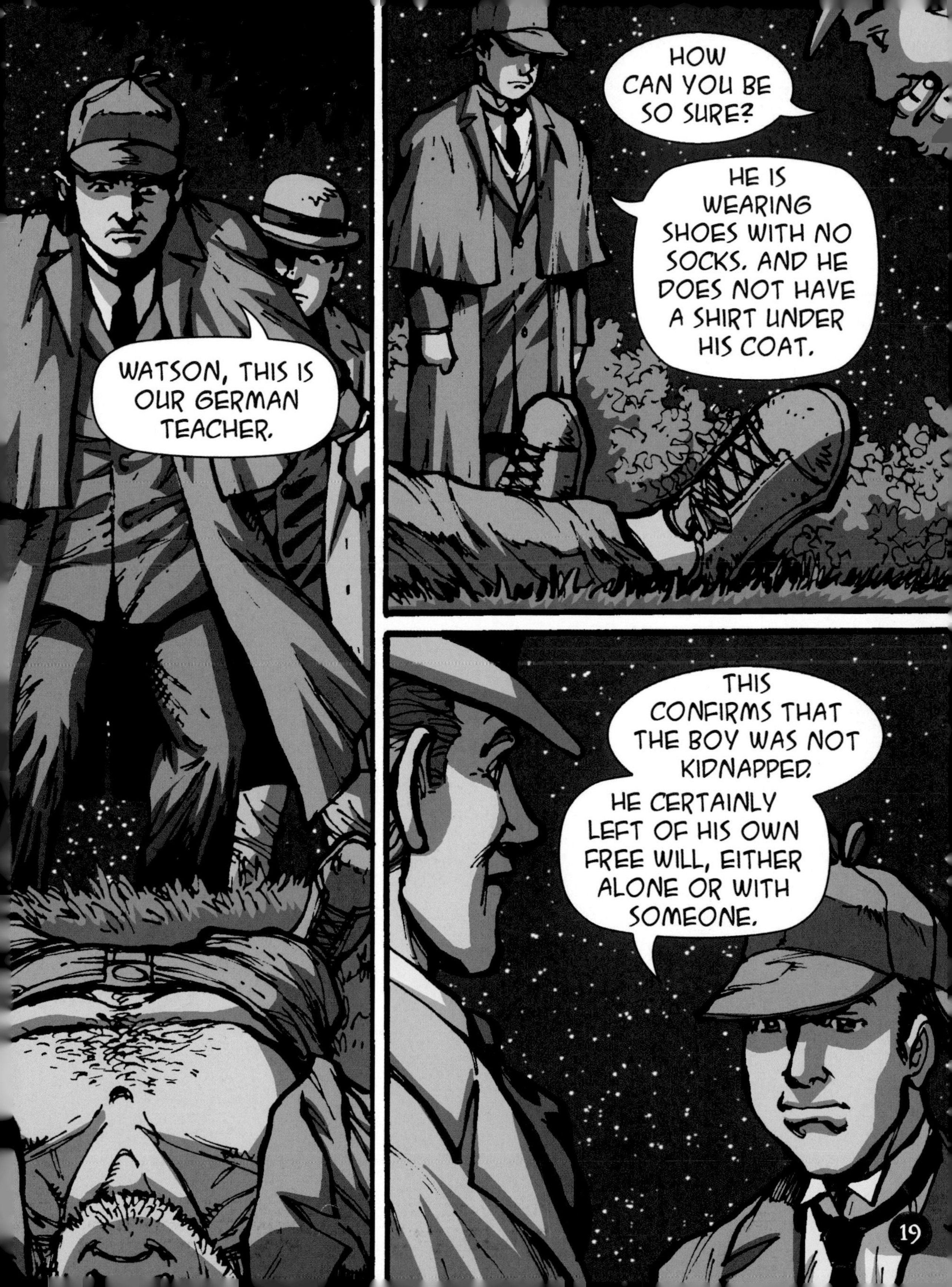
WATSON, THIS IS OUR GERMAN TEACHER.
HOW CAN YOU BE SO SURE?
HE IS WEARING SHOES WITH NO SOCKS. AND HE DOES NOT HAVE A SHIRT UNDER HIS COAT.
THIS CONFIRMS THAT THE BOY WAS NOT KIDNAPPED.
HE CERTAINLY LEFT OF HIS OWN FREE WILL, EITHER ALONE OR WITH SOMEONE.

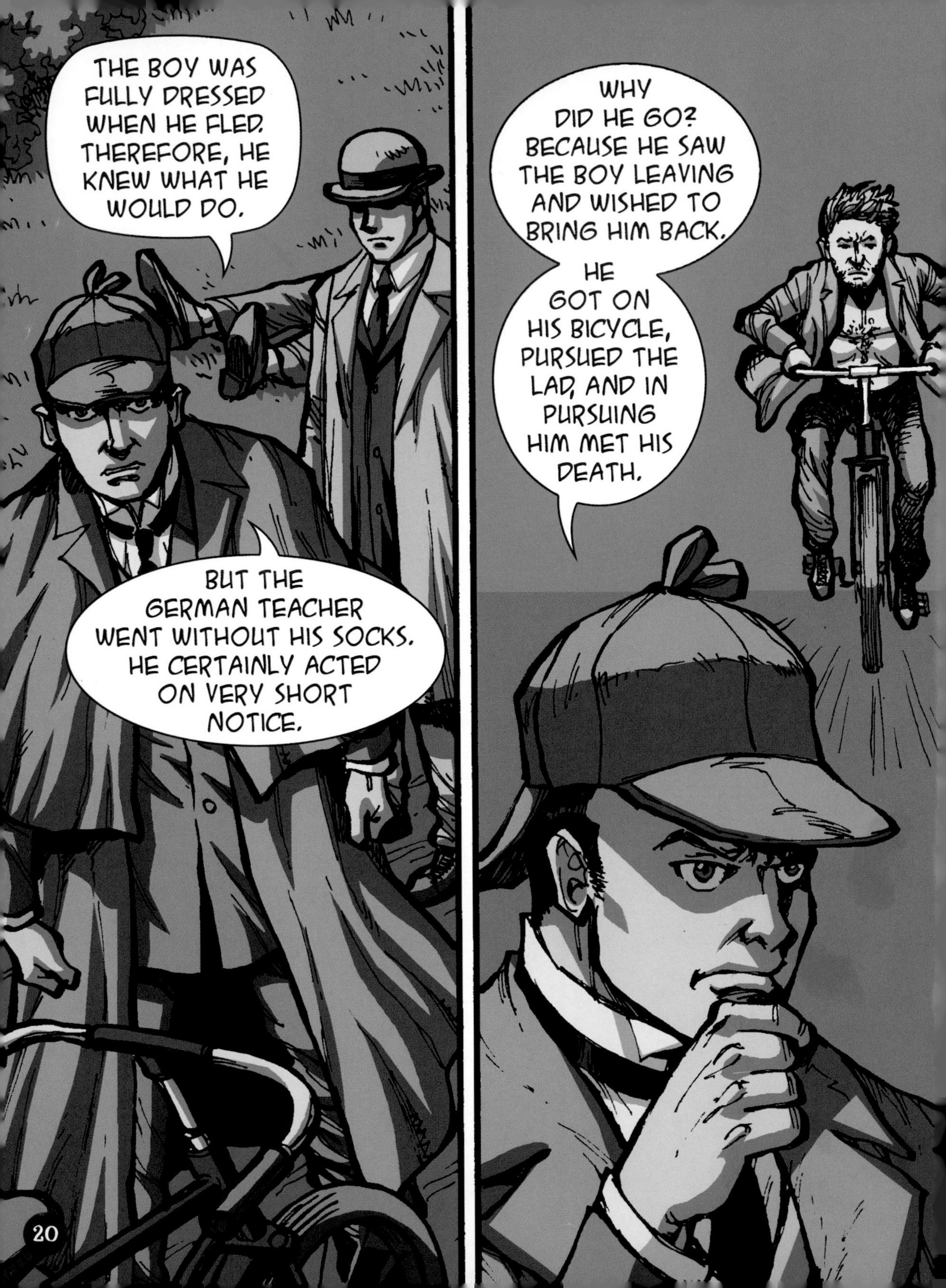
THE BOY WAS FULLY DRESSED WHEN HE FLED. THEREFORE, HE KNEW WHAT HE WOULD DO.
BUT THE GERMAN TEACHER WENT WITHOUT HIS SOCKS. HE CERTAINLY ACTED ON VERY SHORT NOTICE.
WHY DID HE GO? BECAUSE HE SAW THE BOY LEAVING AND WISHED TO BRING HIM BACK.
HE GOT ON HIS BICYCLE, PURSUED THE LAD, AND IN PURSUING HIM MET HIS DEATH.

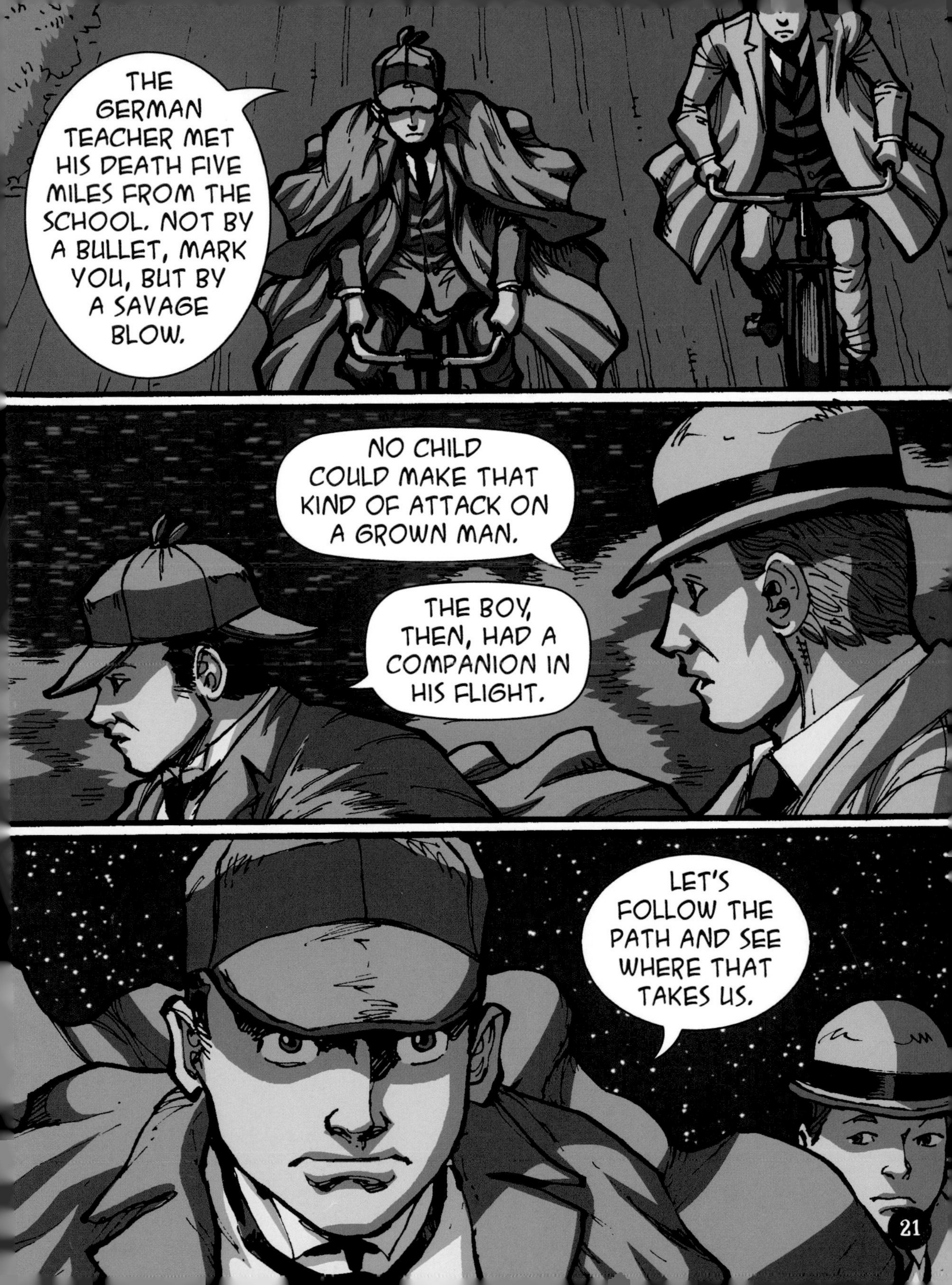
THE GERMAN TEACHER MET HIS DEATH FIVE MILES FROM THE SCHOOL. NOT BY A BULLET, MARK YOU, BUT BY A SAVAGE BLOW.
NO CHILD COULD MAKE THAT KIND OF ATTACK ON A GROWN MAN.
THE BOY, THEN, HAD A COMPANION IN HIS FLIGHT.
LET'S FOLLOW THE PATH AND SEE WHERE THAT TAKES US.

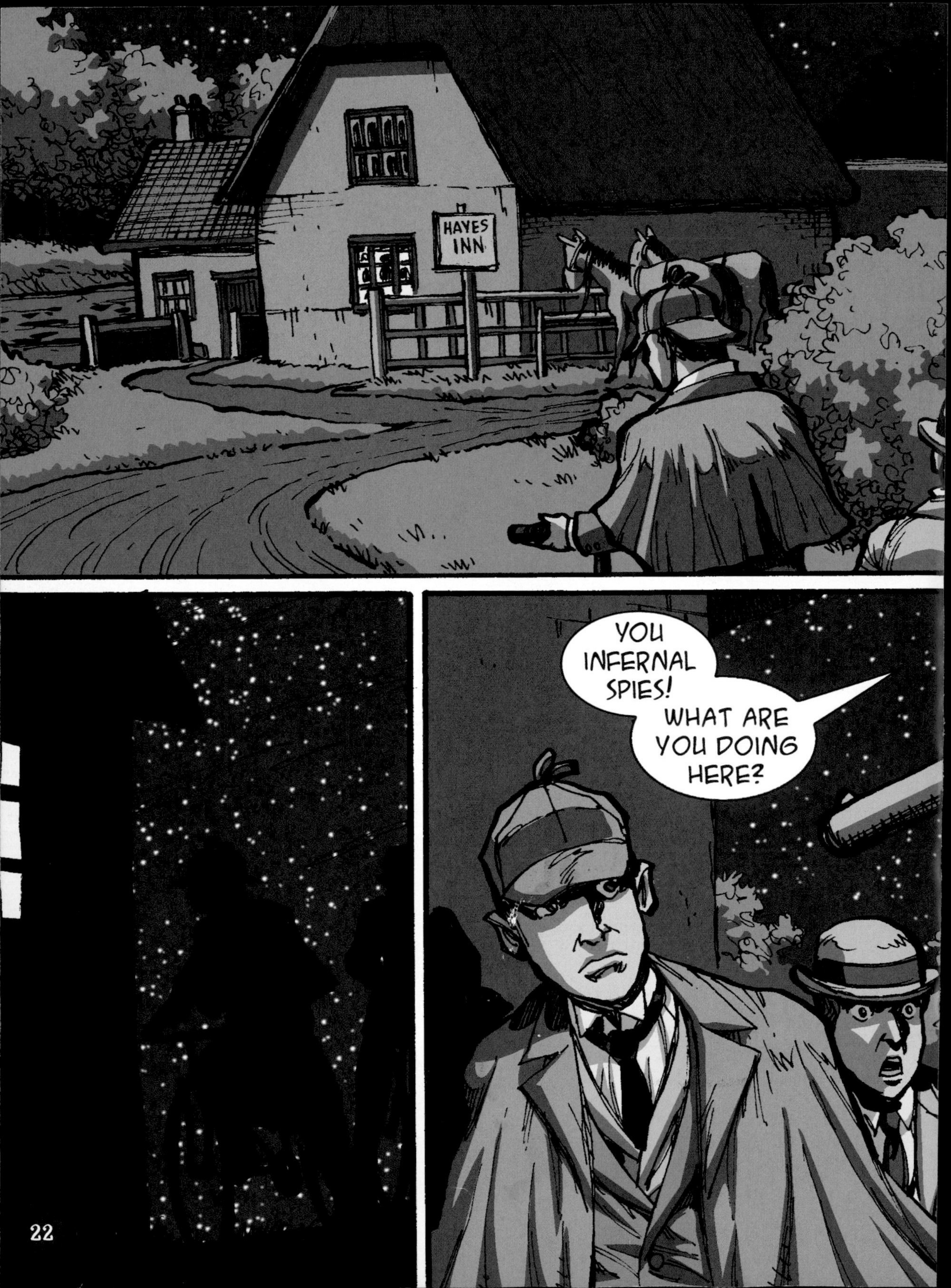
HAYES INN
YOU INFERNAL SPIES!
WHAT ARE YOU DOING HERE?

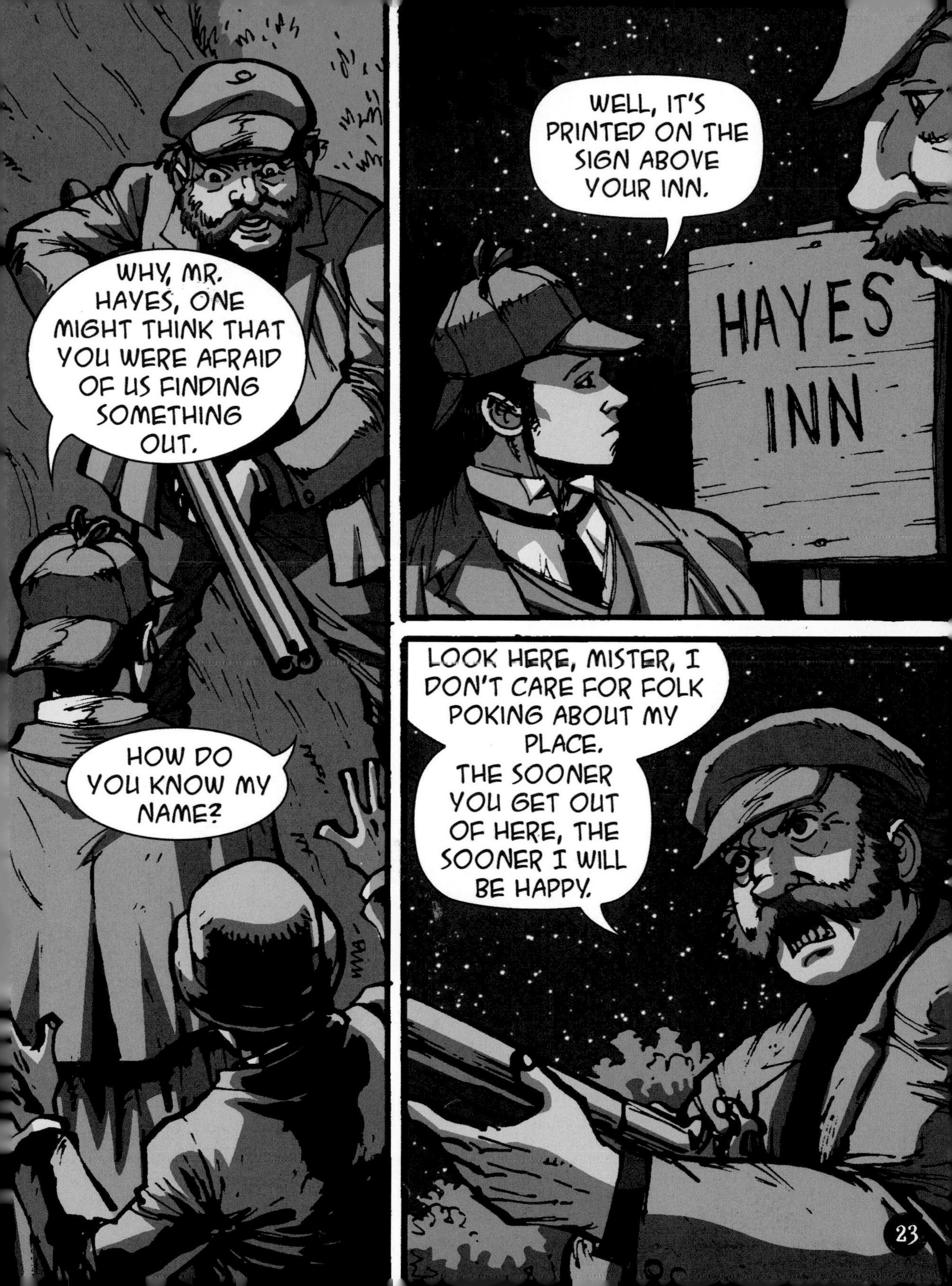
WHY, MR. HAYES, ONE MIGHT THINK THAT YOU WERE AFRAID OF US FINDING SOMETHING OUT.
HOW DO YOU KNOW MY NAME?
WELL, IT'S PRINTED ON THE SIGN ABOVE YOUR INN.
HAYES INN
LOOK HERE, MISTER, I DON'T CARE FOR FOLK POKING ABOUT MY PLACE.
THE SOONER YOU GET OUT OF HERE, THE SOONER I WILL BE HAPPY.

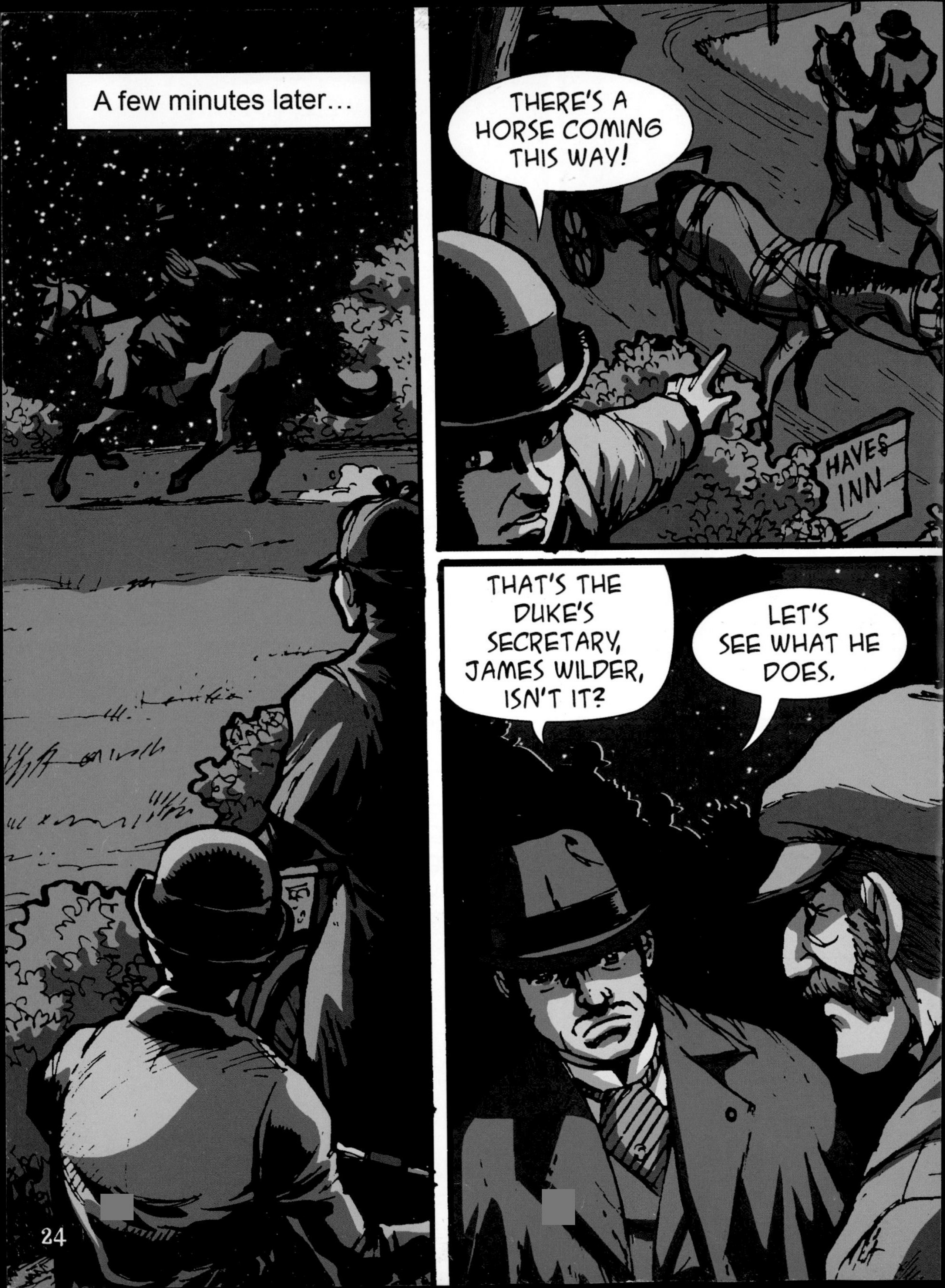
A few minutes later…
THERE'S A HORSE COMING THIS WAY!
HAYES INN
THAT'S THE DUKE'S SECRETARY, JAMES WILDER, ISN'T IT?
LET'S SEE WHAT HE DOES.

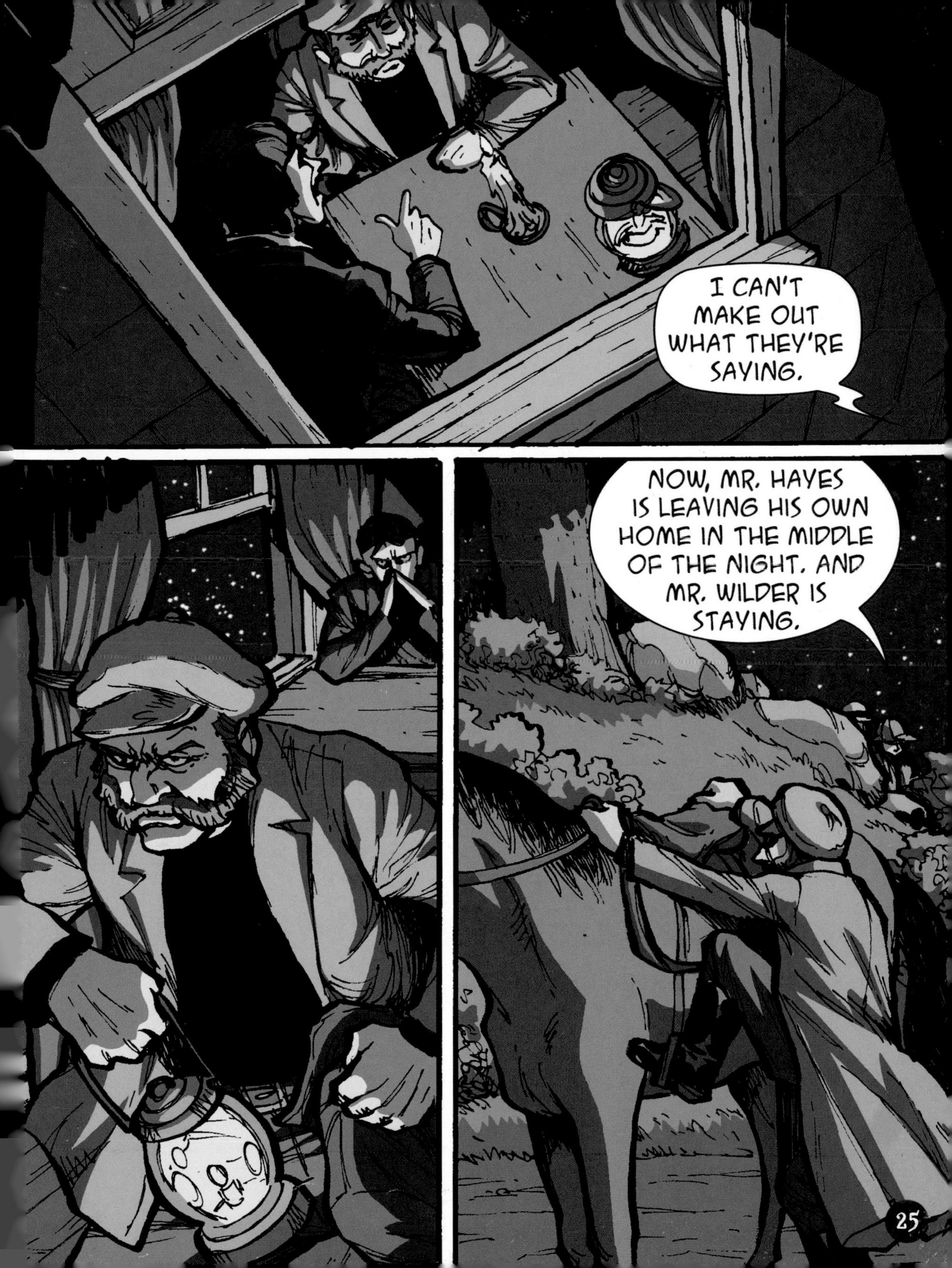
I CAN'T MAKE OUT WHAT THEY'RE SAYING.
NOW, MR. HAYES IS LEAVING HIS OWN HOME IN THE MIDDLE OF THE NIGHT. AND MR. WILDER IS STAYING.

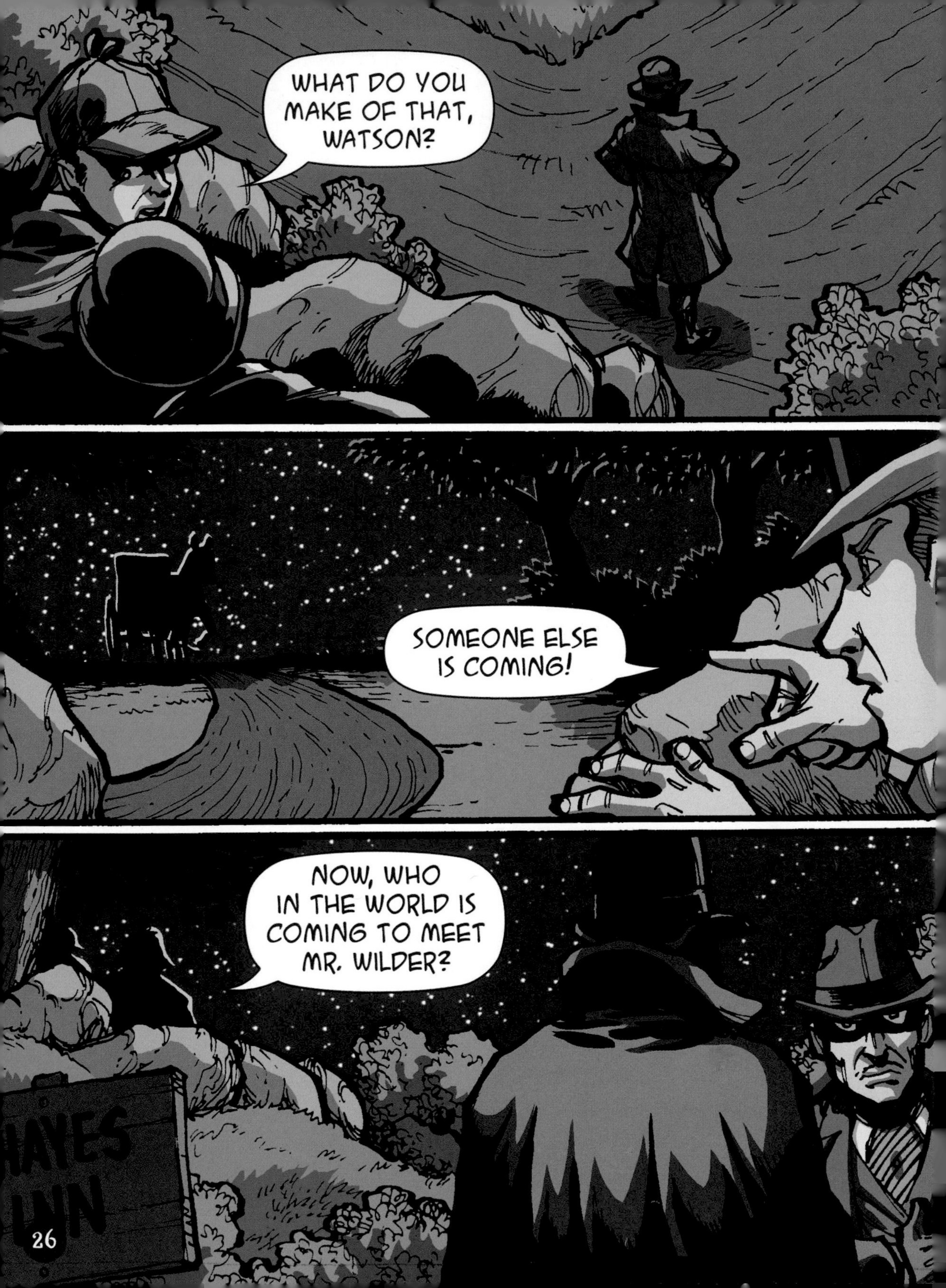

WHAT DO YOU MAKE OF THAT, WATSON?
SOMEONE ELSE IS COMING!
NOW, WHO IN THE WORLD IS COMING TO MEET MR. WILDER?
HAYES INN

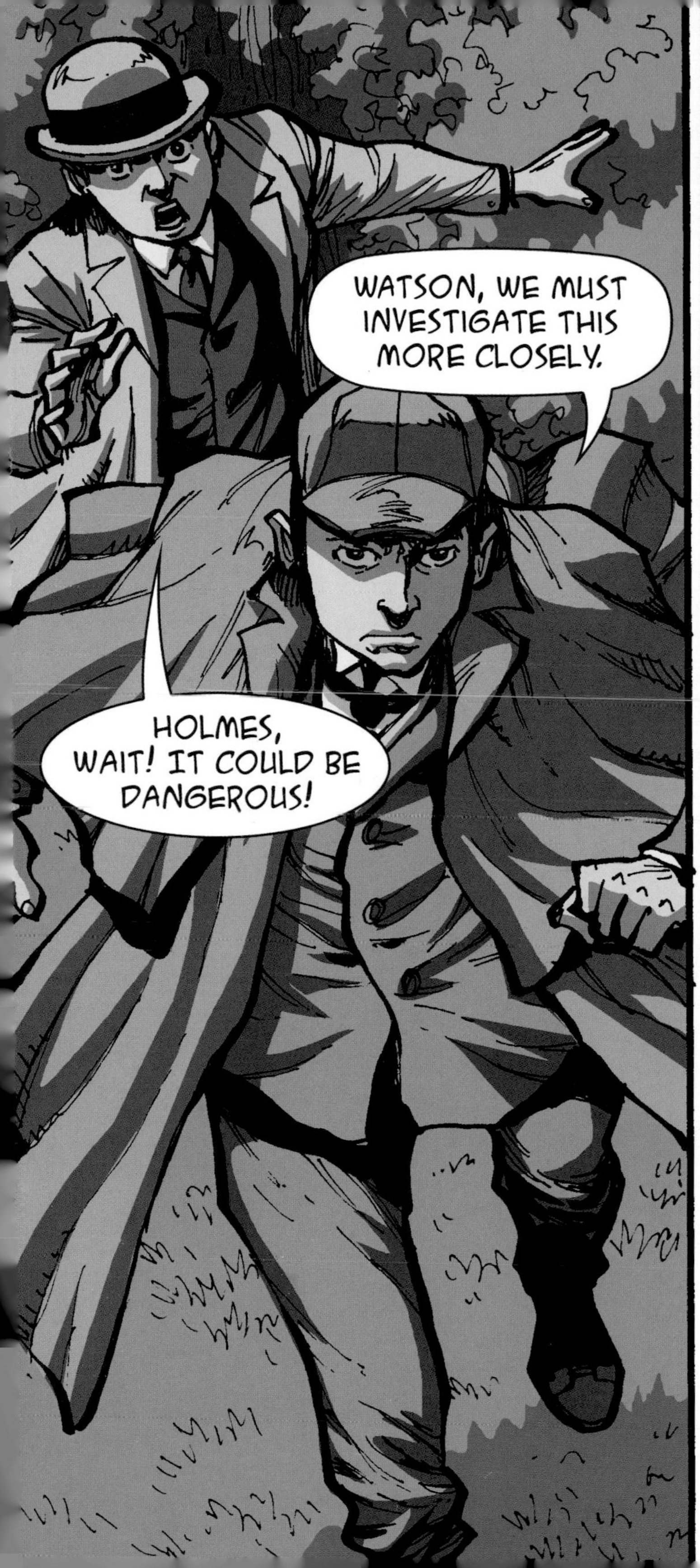
WATSON, WE MUST INVESTIGATE THIS MORE CLOSELY.
HOLMES, WAIT! IT COULD BE DANGEROUS!
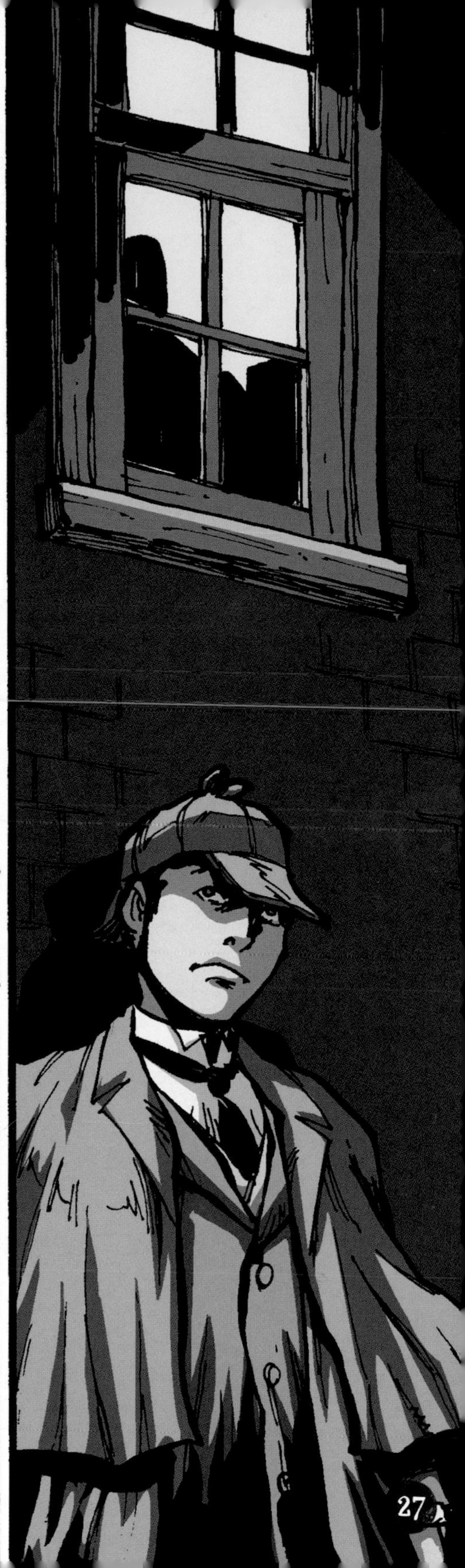

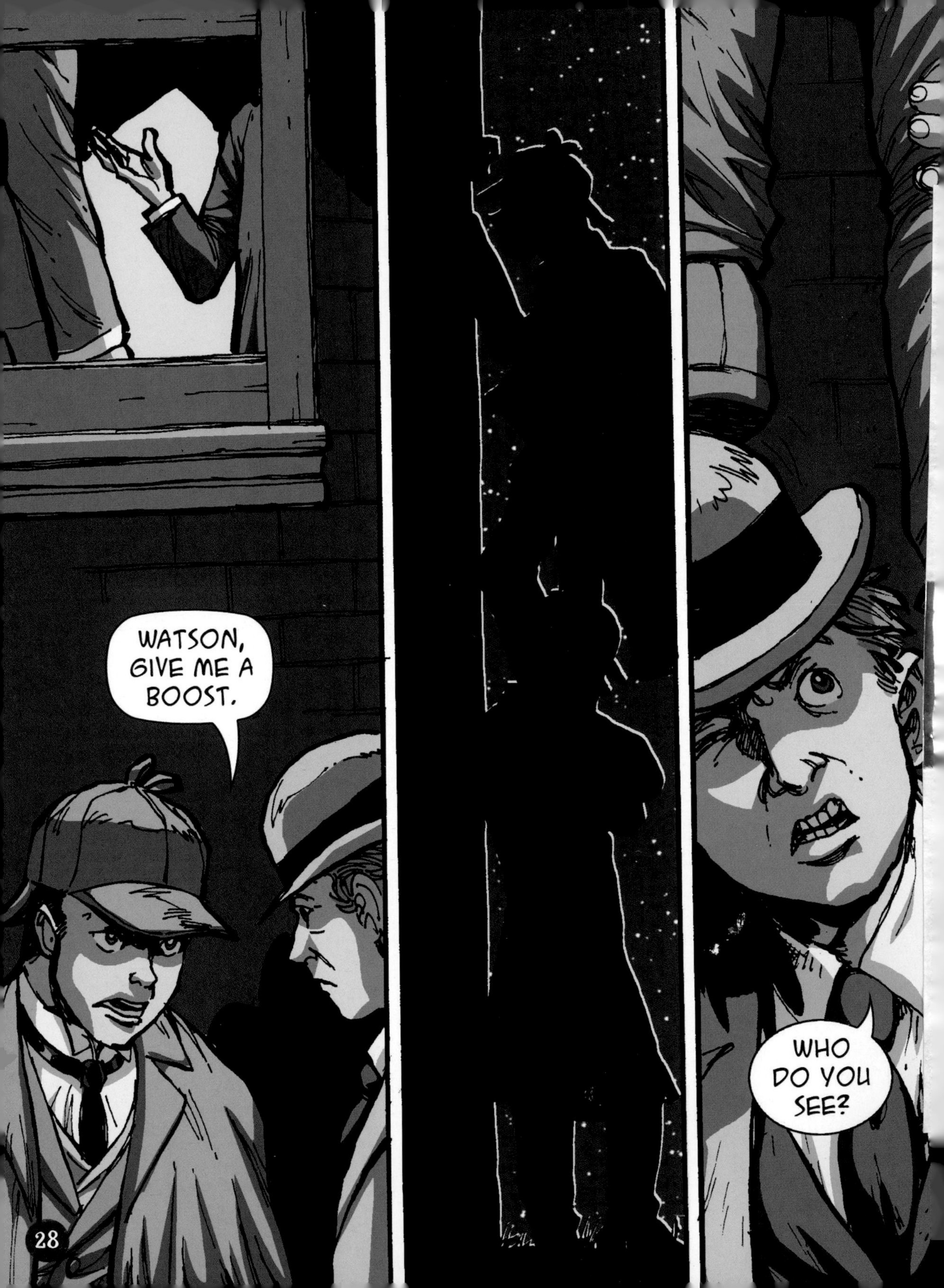
WATSON, GIVE ME A BOOST.
WHO DO YOU SEE?

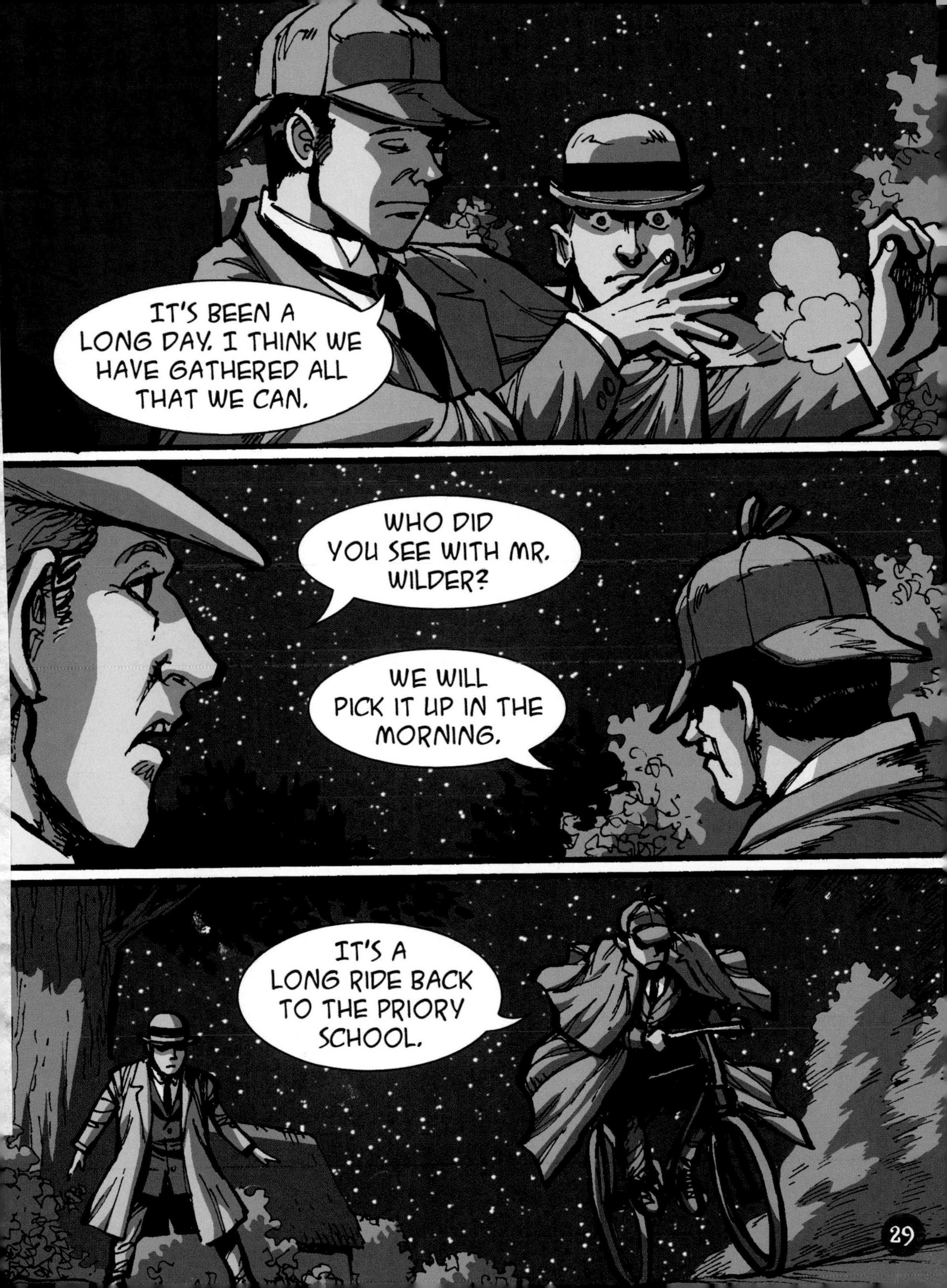
IT'S BEEN A LONG DAY. I THINK WE HAVE GATHERED ALL THAT WE CAN.
WHO DID YOU SEE WITH MR. WILDER?
WE WILL PICK IT UP IN THE MORNING.
IT'S A LONG RIDE BACK TO THE PRIORY SCHOOL.

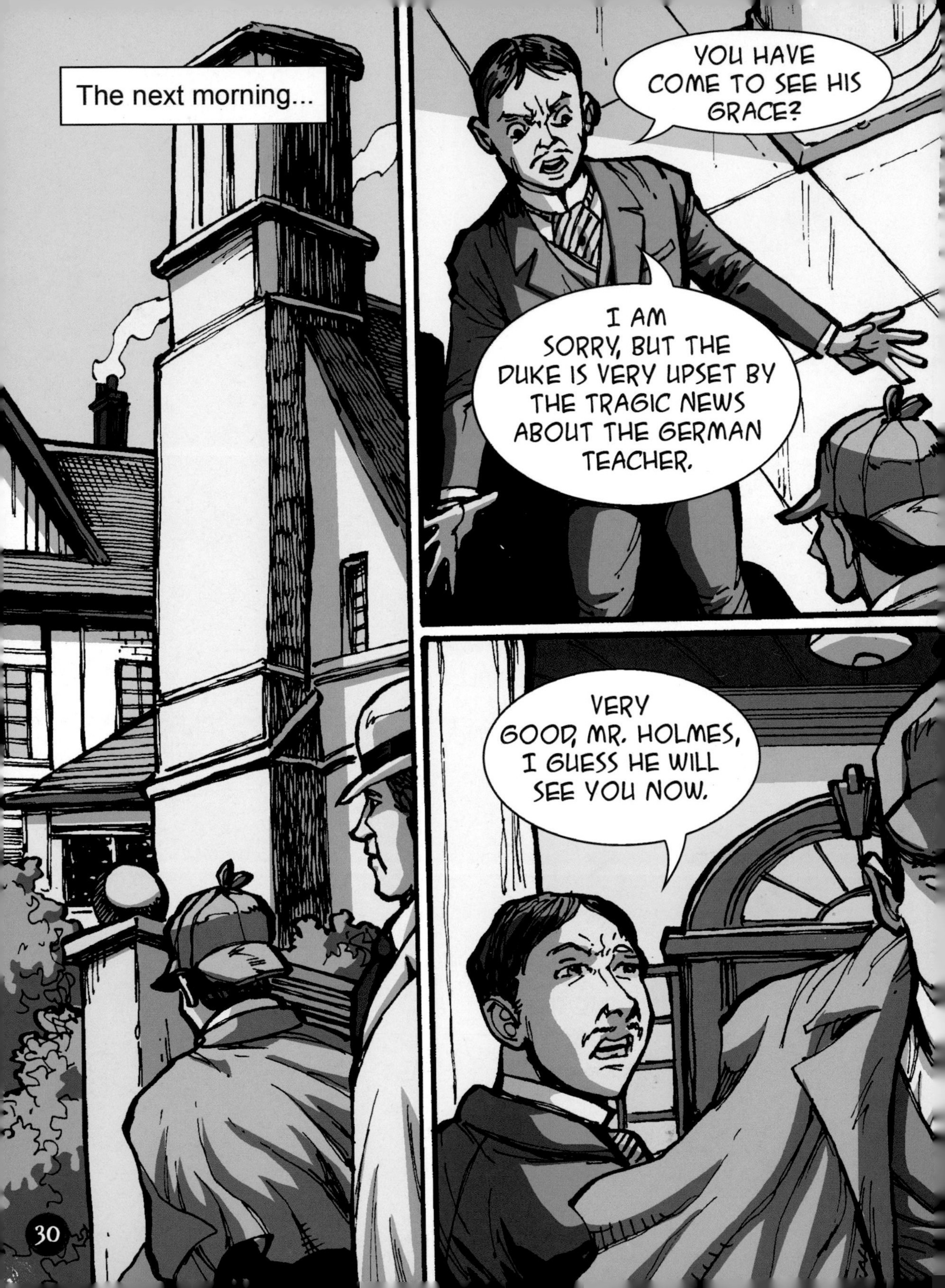
The next morning...
YOU HAVE COME TO SEE HIS GRACE?
I AM SORRY, BUT THE DUKE IS VERY UPSET BY THE TRAGIC NEWS ABOUT THE GERMAN TEACHER.
VERY GOOD, MR. HOLMES, I GUESS HE WILL SEE YOU NOW.

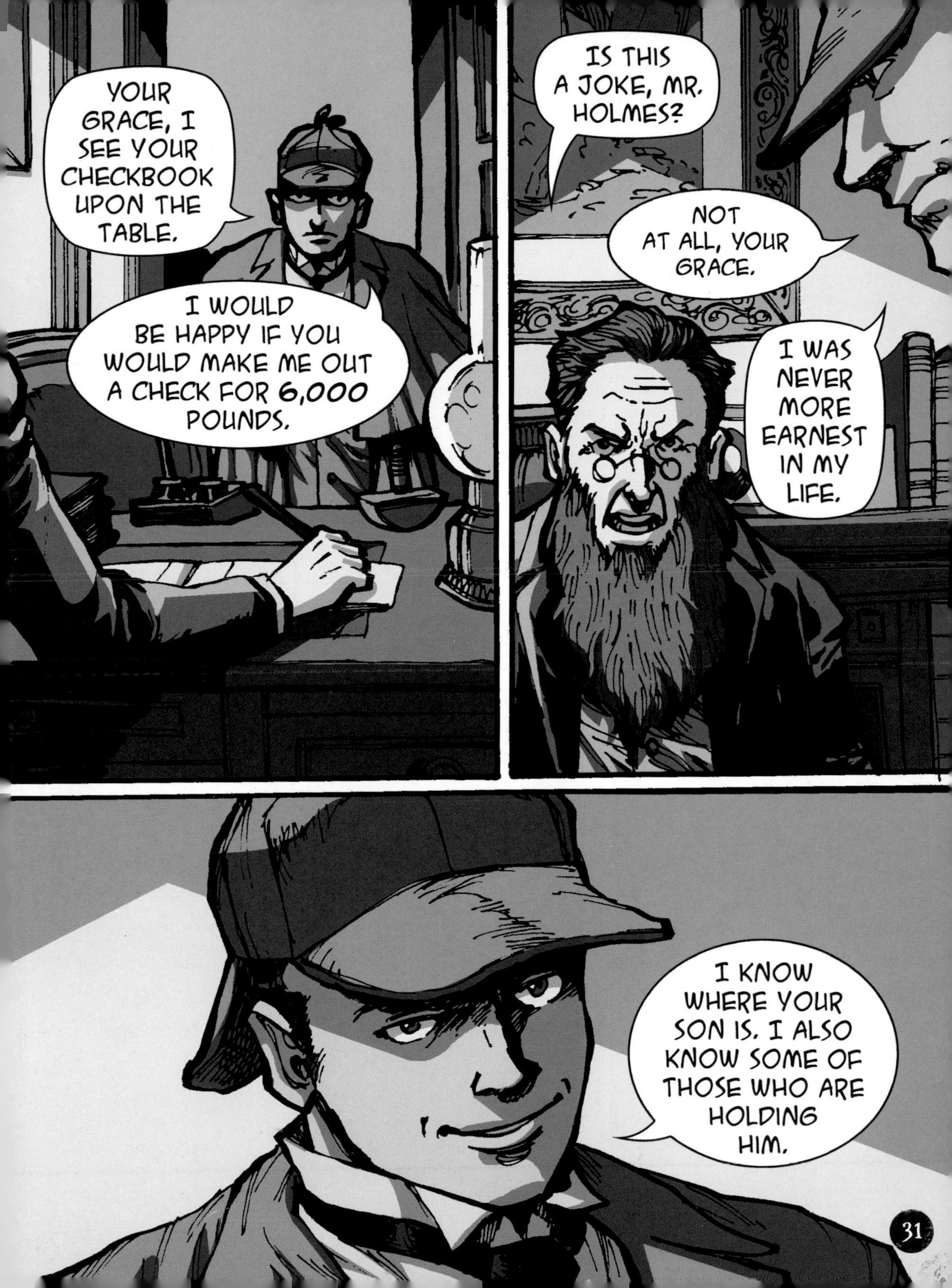
YOUR GRACE, I SEE YOUR CHECKBOOK UPON THE TABLE.
I WOULD BE HAPPY IF YOU WOULD MAKE ME OUT A CHECK FOR 6,000 POUNDS.
IS THIS A JOKE, MR. HOLMES?
NOT AT ALL, YOUR GRACE.
I WAS NEVER MORE EARNEST IN MY LIFE.
I KNOW WHERE YOUR SON IS. I ALSO KNOW SOME OF THOSE WHO ARE HOLDING HIM.

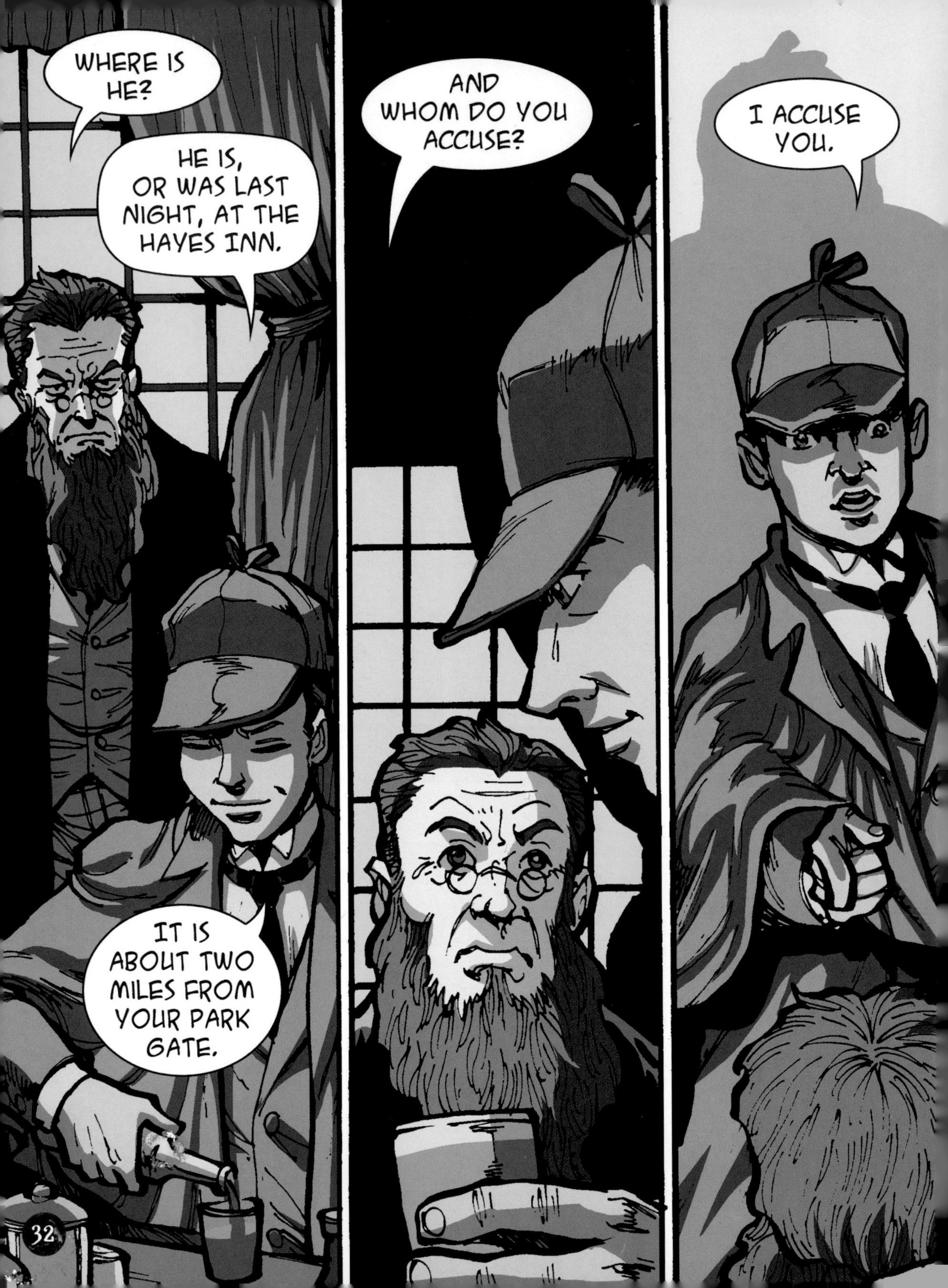
WHERE IS HE?
HE IS, OR WAS LAST NIGHT, AT THE HAYES INN.
IT IS ABOUT TWO MILES FROM YOUR PARK GATE.
AND WHOM DO YOU ACCUSE?
I ACCUSE YOU.

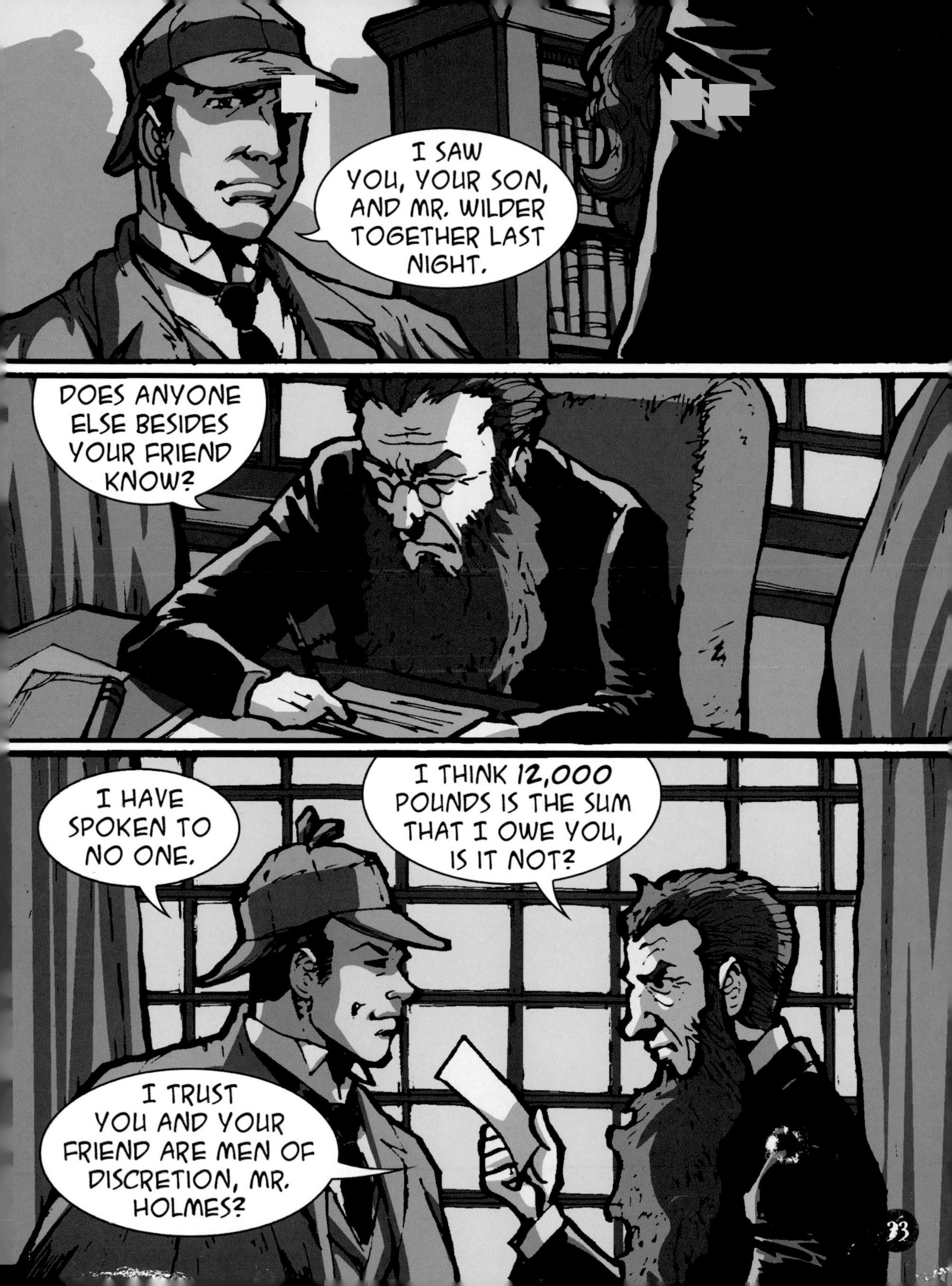
I SAW YOU, YOUR SON, AND MR. WILDER TOGETHER LAST NIGHT.
DOES ANYONE ELSE BESIDES YOUR FRIEND KNOW?
I HAVE SPOKEN TO NO ONE.
I THINK 12,000 POUNDS IS THE SUM THAT I OWE YOU, IS IT NOT?
I TRUST YOU AND YOUR FRIEND ARE MEN OF DISCRETION, MR. HOLMES?

I FEAR, YOUR GRACE, THAT MATTERS CAN HARDLY BE ARRANGED SO EASILY. THERE IS THE DEATH OF THE GERMAN TEACHER.

THAT WAS THE WORK OF THE HORRIBLE RUFFIAN WHOM MR. WILDER HAD THE MISFORTUNE TO EMPLOY.

WHY DID MR. WILDER HIRE MR. HAYES?

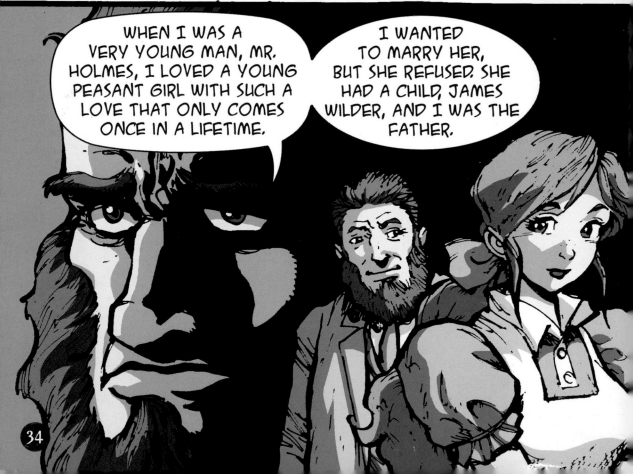

WHEN I WAS A VERY YOUNG MAN, MR. HOLMES, I LOVED A YOUNG PEASANT GIRL WITH SUCH A LOVE THAT ONLY COMES ONCE IN A LIFETIME.

I WANTED TO MARRY HER, BUT SHE REFUSED. SHE HAD A CHILD, JAMES WILDER, AND I WAS THE FATHER.

34

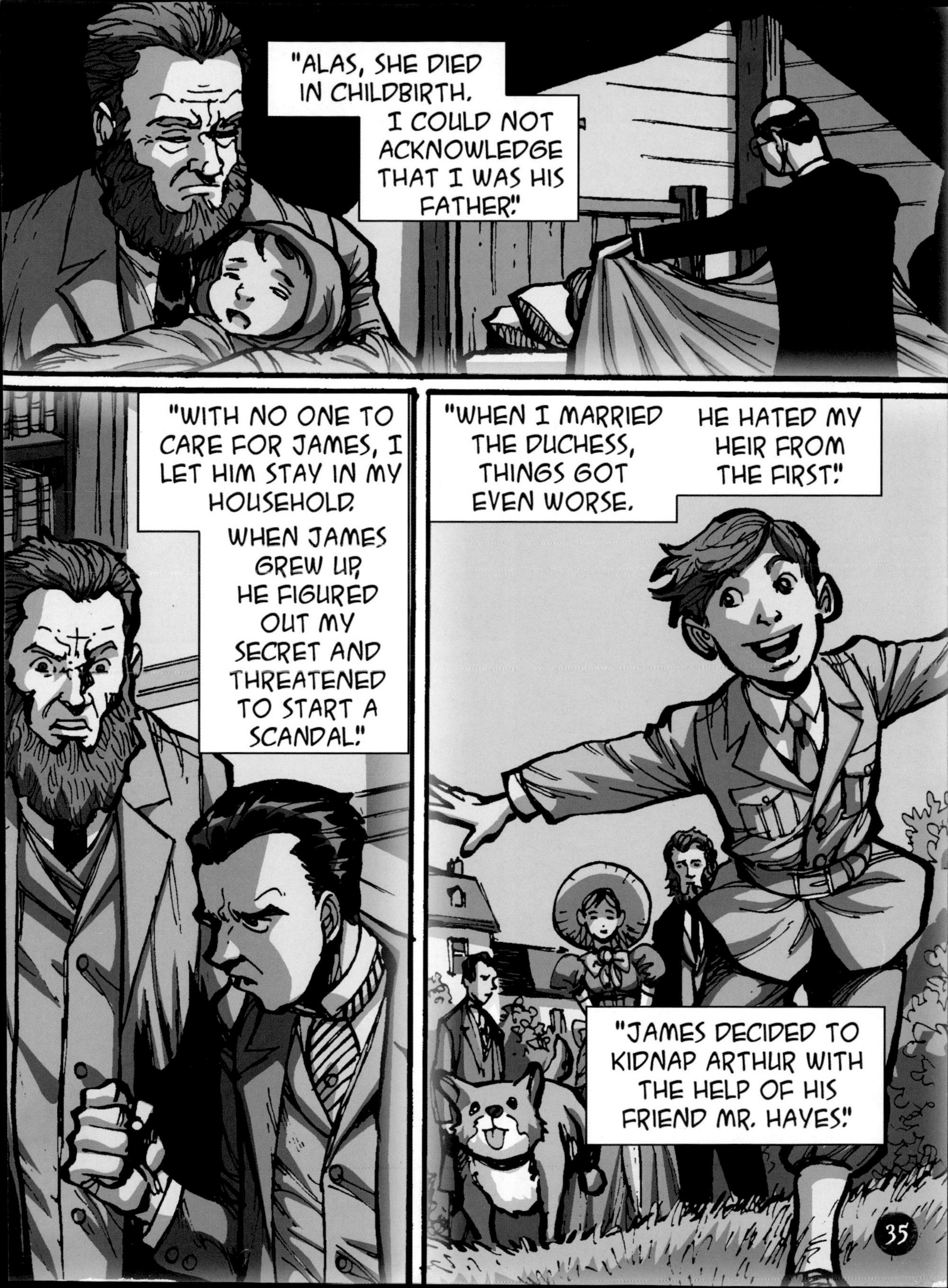
"ALAS, SHE DIED IN CHILDBIRTH.
I COULD NOT ACKNOWLEDGE THAT I WAS HIS FATHER."
"WITH NO ONE TO CARE FOR JAMES, I LET HIM STAY IN MY HOUSEHOLD.
WHEN JAMES GREW UP, HE FIGURED OUT MY SECRET AND THREATENED TO START A SCANDAL."
"WHEN I MARRIED THE DUCHESS, THINGS GOT EVEN WORSE.
HE HATED MY HEIR FROM THE FIRST."
"JAMES DECIDED TO KIDNAP ARTHUR WITH THE HELP OF HIS FRIEND MR. HAYES."

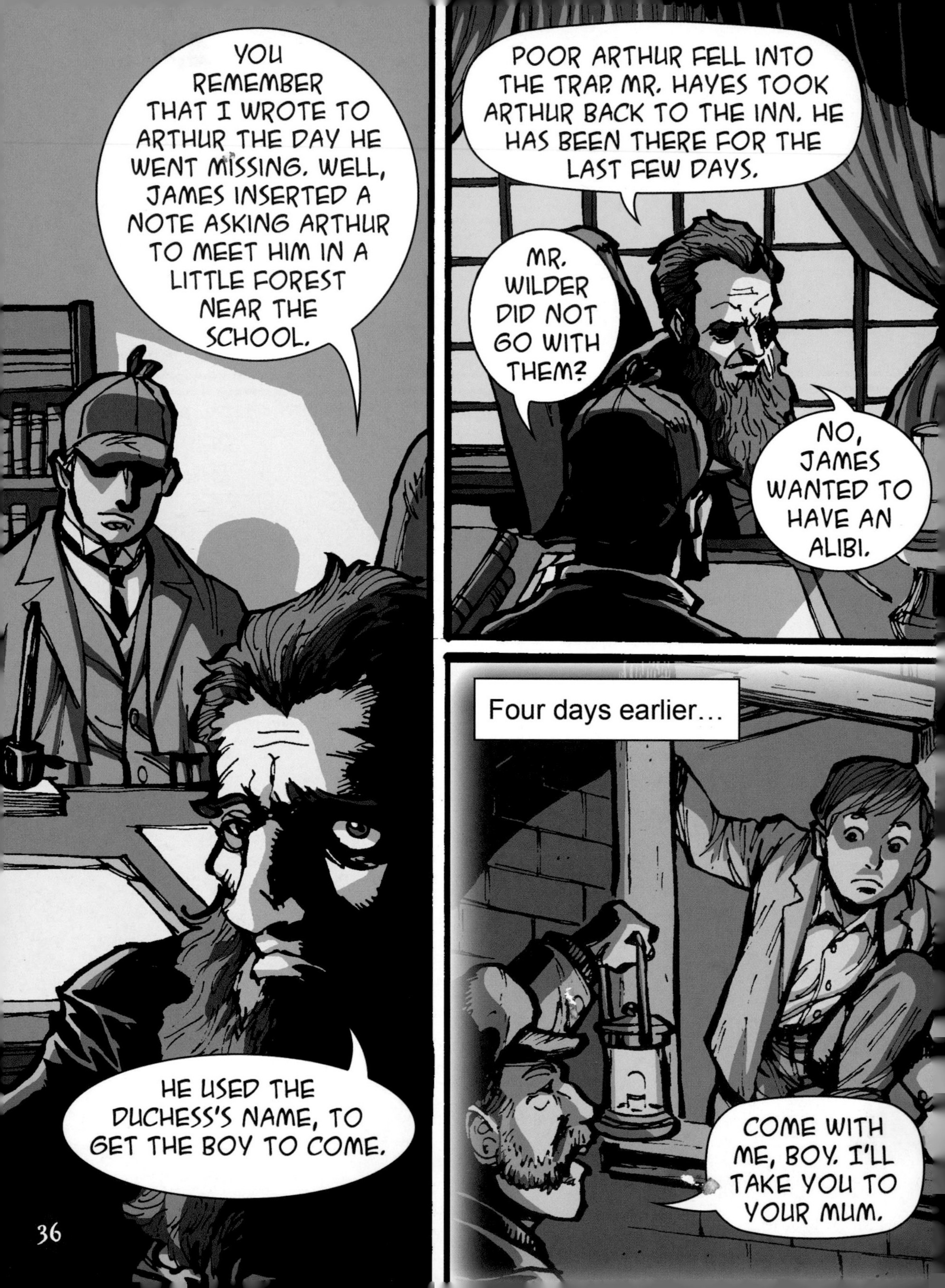
YOU REMEMBER THAT I WROTE TO ARTHUR THE DAY HE WENT MISSING. WELL, JAMES INSERTED A NOTE ASKING ARTHUR TO MEET HIM IN A LITTLE FOREST NEAR THE SCHOOL.
HE USED THE DUCHESS'S NAME, TO GET THE BOY TO COME.
POOR ARTHUR FELL INTO THE TRAP. MR. HAYES TOOK ARTHUR BACK TO THE INN. HE HAS BEEN THERE FOR THE LAST FEW DAYS.
MR. WILDER DID NOT GO WITH THEM?
NO, JAMES WANTED TO HAVE AN ALIBI.
Four days earlier…
COME WITH ME, BOY. I'LL TAKE YOU TO YOUR MUM.

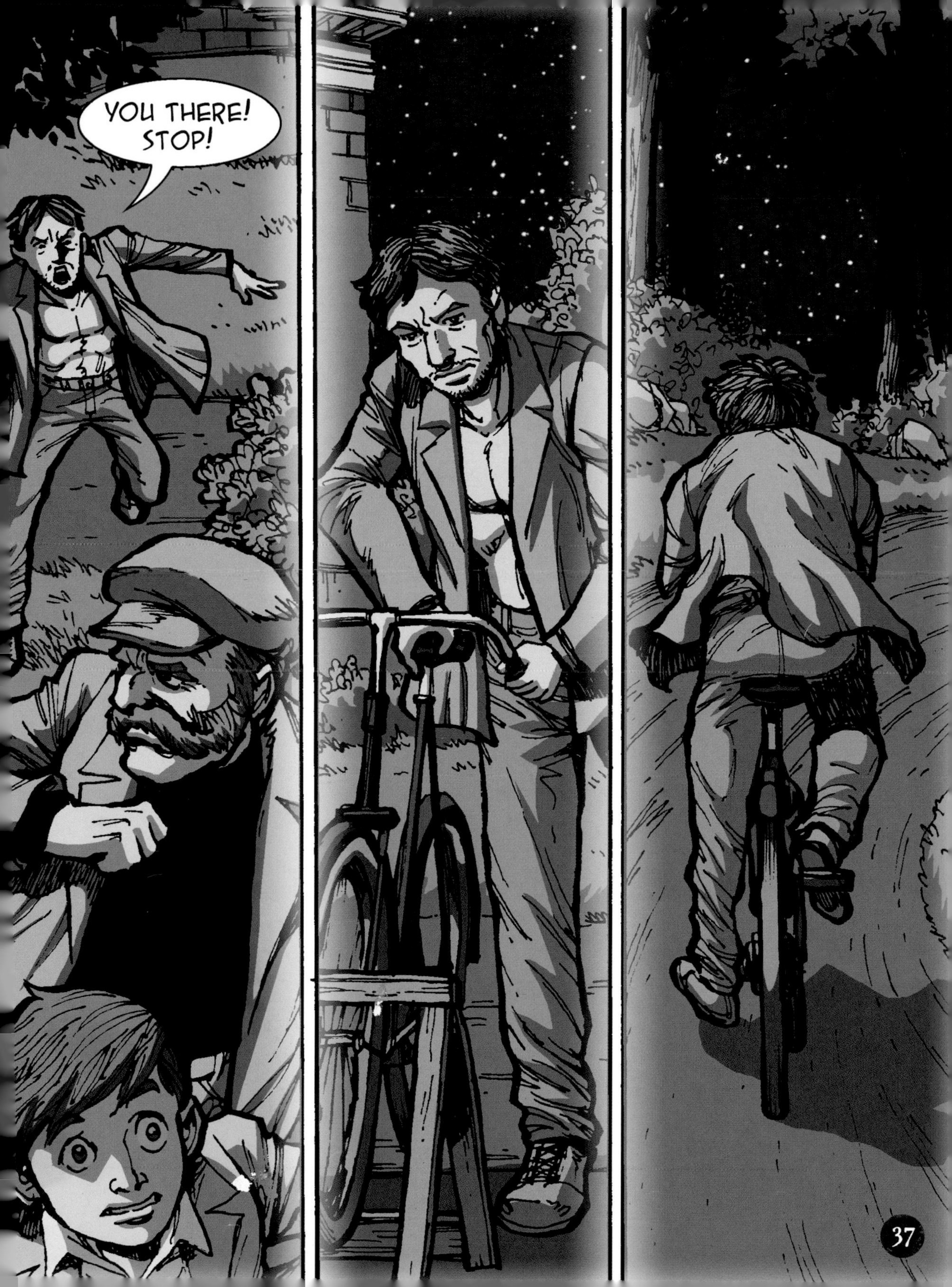
YOU THERE! STOP!

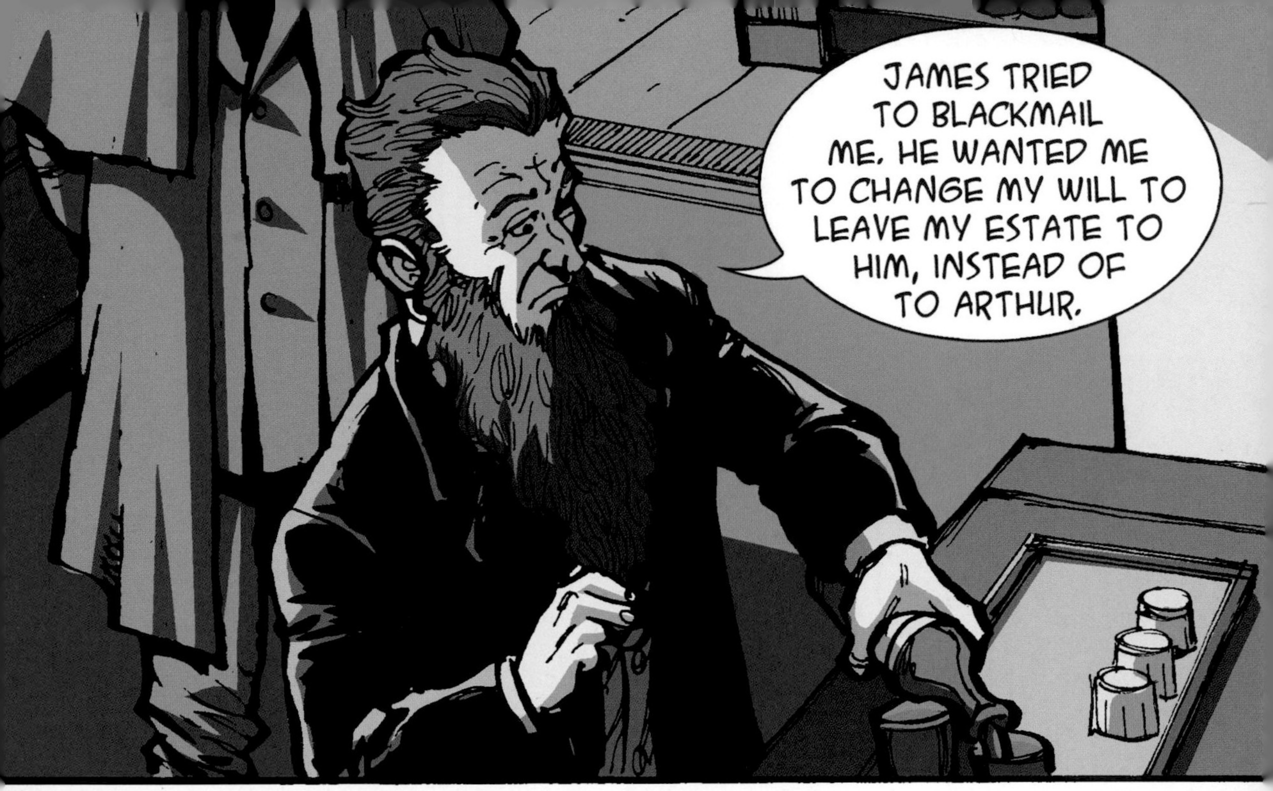
JAMES TRIED TO BLACKMAIL ME. HE WANTED ME TO CHANGE MY WILL TO LEAVE MY ESTATE TO HIM, INSTEAD OF TO ARTHUR.

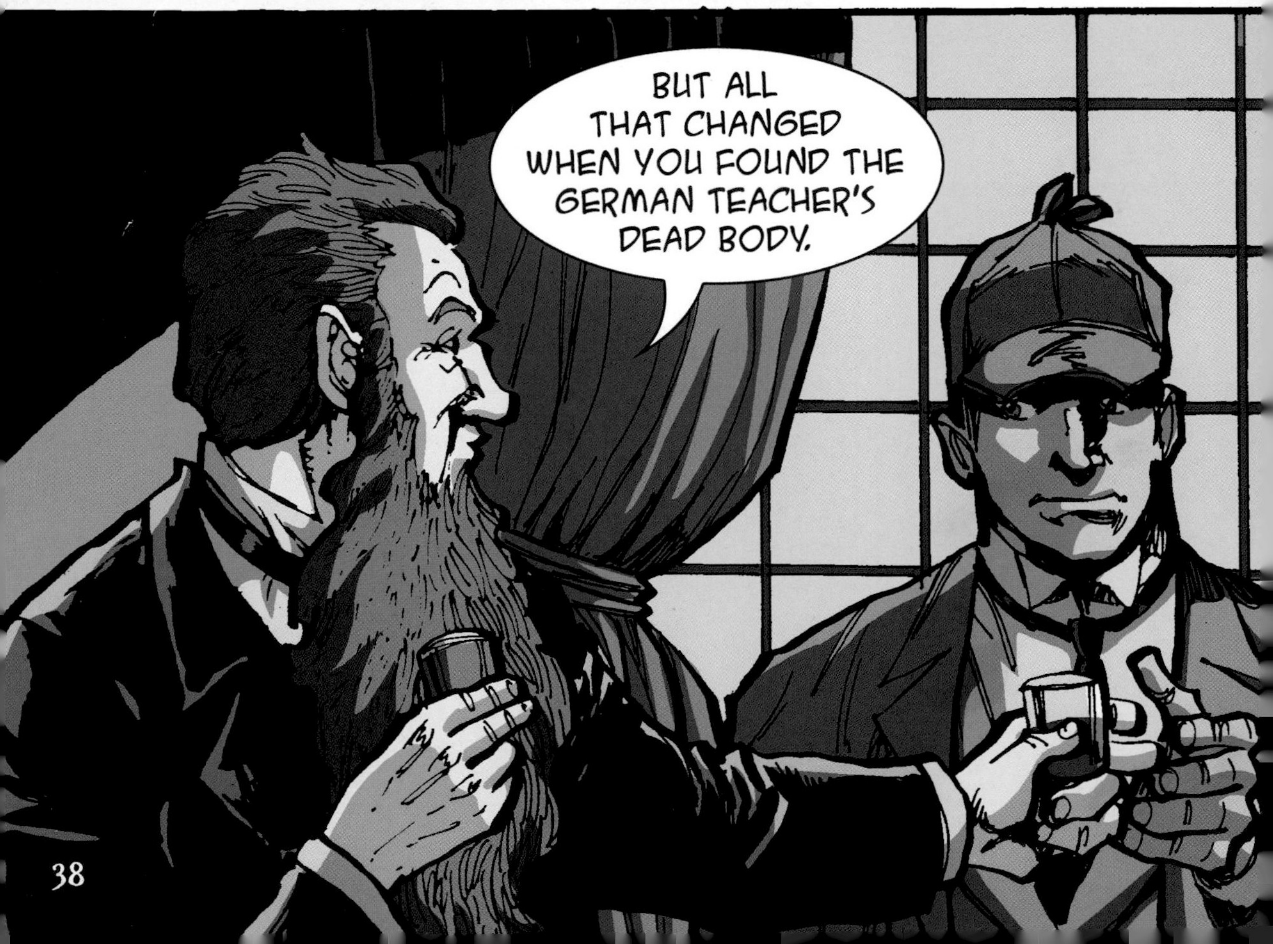
BUT ALL THAT CHANGED WHEN YOU FOUND THE GERMAN TEACHER'S DEAD BODY.

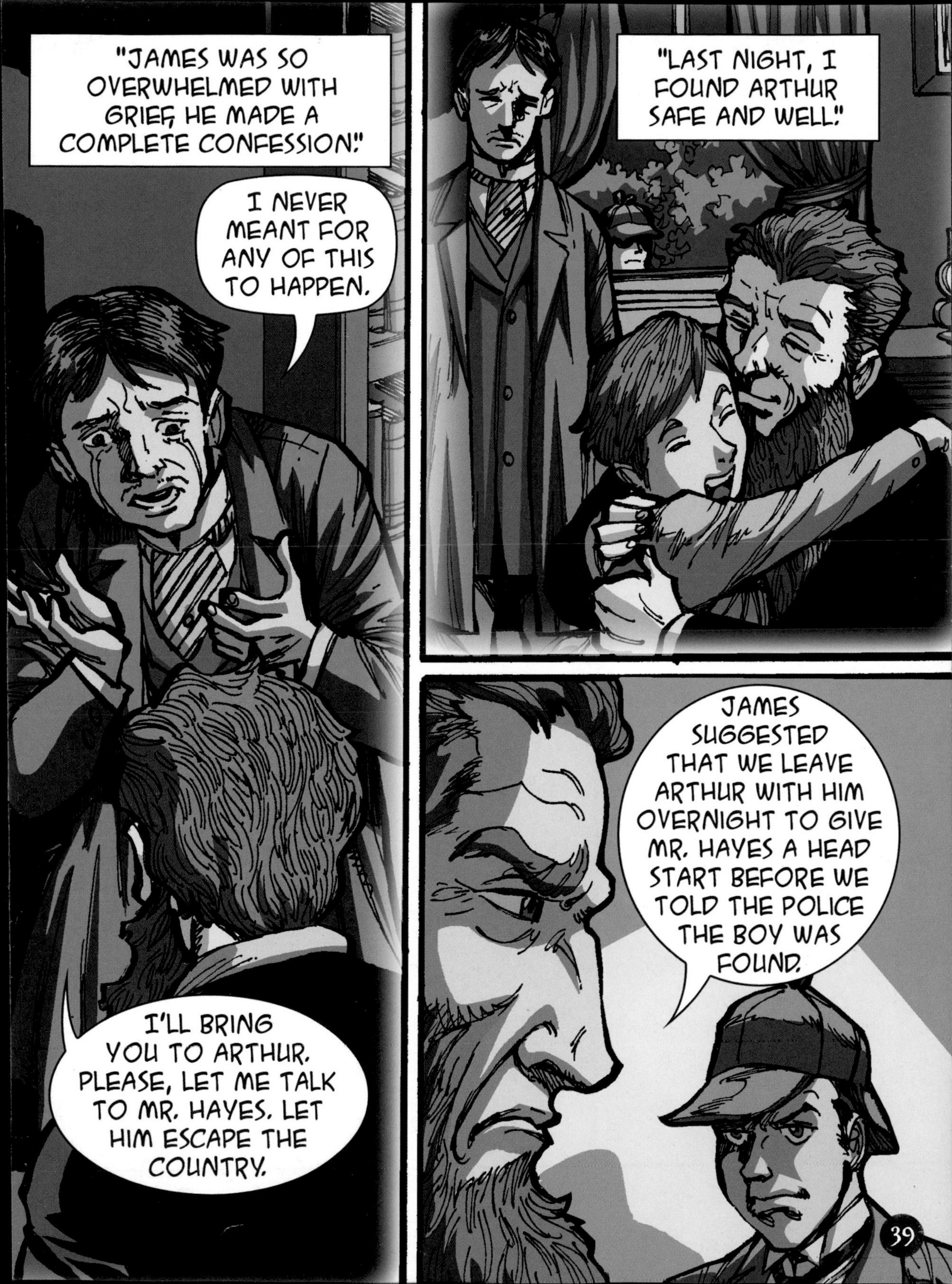
"JAMES WAS SO OVERWHELMED WITH GRIEF, HE MADE A COMPLETE CONFESSION."
I NEVER MEANT FOR ANY OF THIS TO HAPPEN.
I'LL BRING YOU TO ARTHUR. PLEASE, LET ME TALK TO MR. HAYES. LET HIM ESCAPE THE COUNTRY.
"LAST NIGHT, I FOUND ARTHUR SAFE AND WELL."
JAMES SUGGESTED THAT WE LEAVE ARTHUR WITH HIM OVERNIGHT TO GIVE MR. HAYES A HEAD START BEFORE WE TOLD THE POLICE THE BOY WAS FOUND.

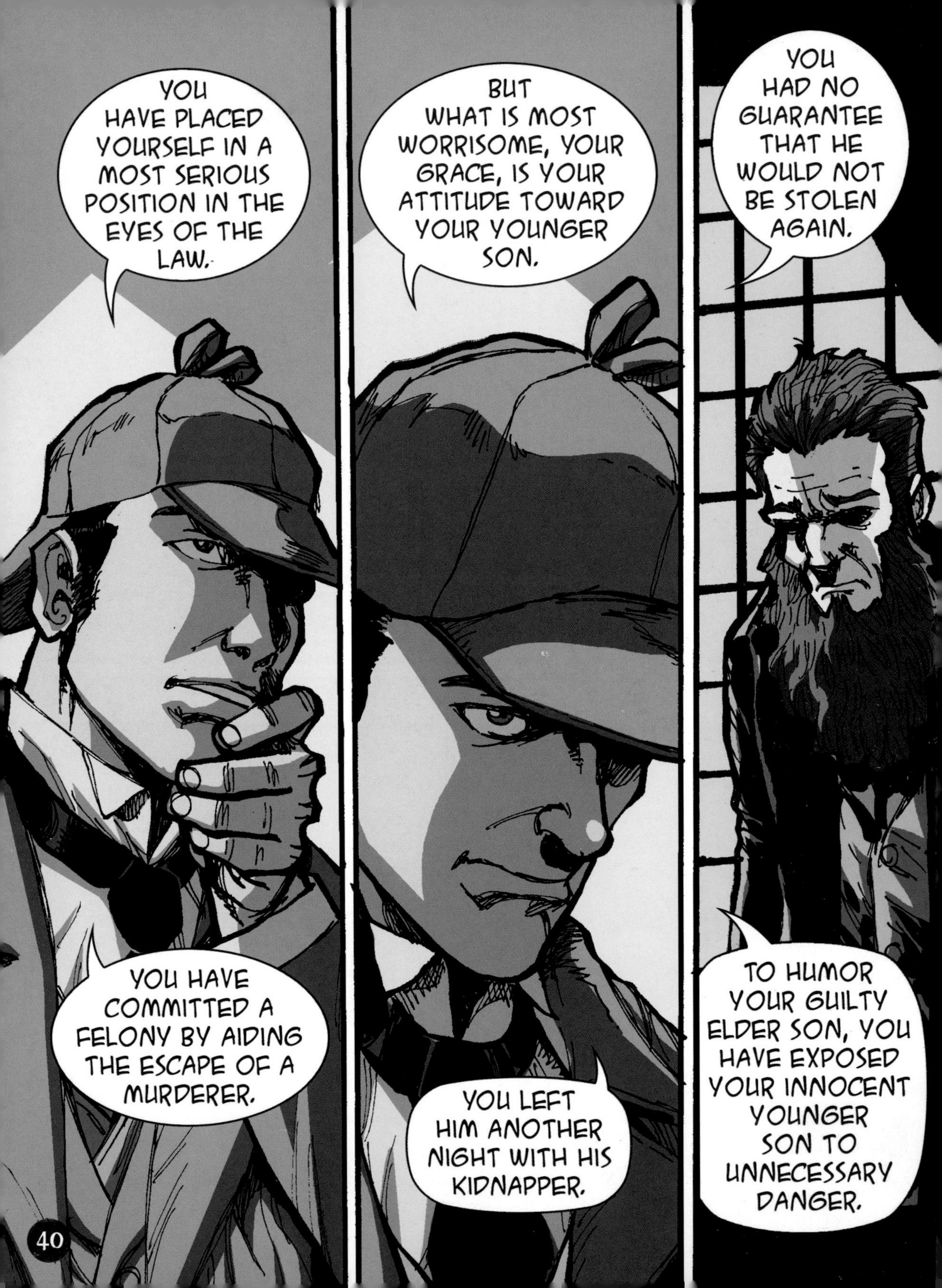
YOU HAVE PLACED YOURSELF IN A MOST SERIOUS POSITION IN THE EYES OF THE LAW.
YOU HAVE COMMITTED A FELONY BY AIDING THE ESCAPE OF A MURDERER.
BUT WHAT IS MOST WORRISOME, YOUR GRACE, IS YOUR ATTITUDE TOWARD YOUR YOUNGER SON.
YOU LEFT HIM ANOTHER NIGHT WITH HIS KIDNAPPER.
YOU HAD NO GUARANTEE THAT HE WOULD NOT BE STOLEN AGAIN.
TO HUMOR YOUR GUILTY ELDER SON, YOU HAVE EXPOSED YOUR INNOCENT YOUNGER SON TO UNNECESSARY DANGER.

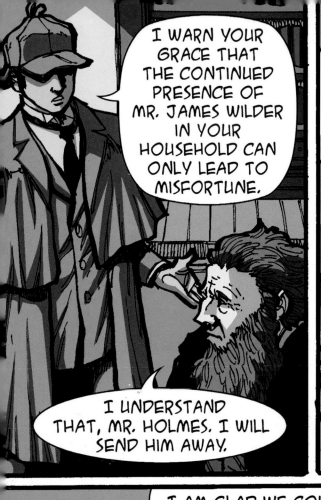

I WARN YOUR GRACE THAT THE CONTINUED PRESENCE OF MR. JAMES WILDER IN YOUR HOUSEHOLD CAN ONLY LEAD TO MISFORTUNE.

I UNDERSTAND THAT, MR. HOLMES. I WILL SEND HIM AWAY.

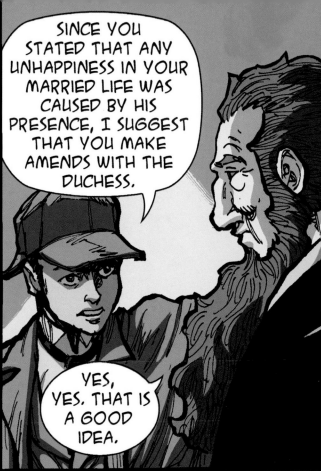

SINCE YOU STATED THAT ANY UNHAPPINESS IN YOUR MARRIED LIFE WAS CAUSED BY HIS PRESENCE, I SUGGEST THAT YOU MAKE AMENDS WITH THE DUCHESS.

YES, YES. THAT IS A GOOD IDEA.

I AM GLAD WE COULD SOLVE THE CASE FOR YOU.

THAT IS THE SECOND PIECE OF GOOD NEWS I HAVE HEARD TODAY.

WHAT WAS THE FIRST?

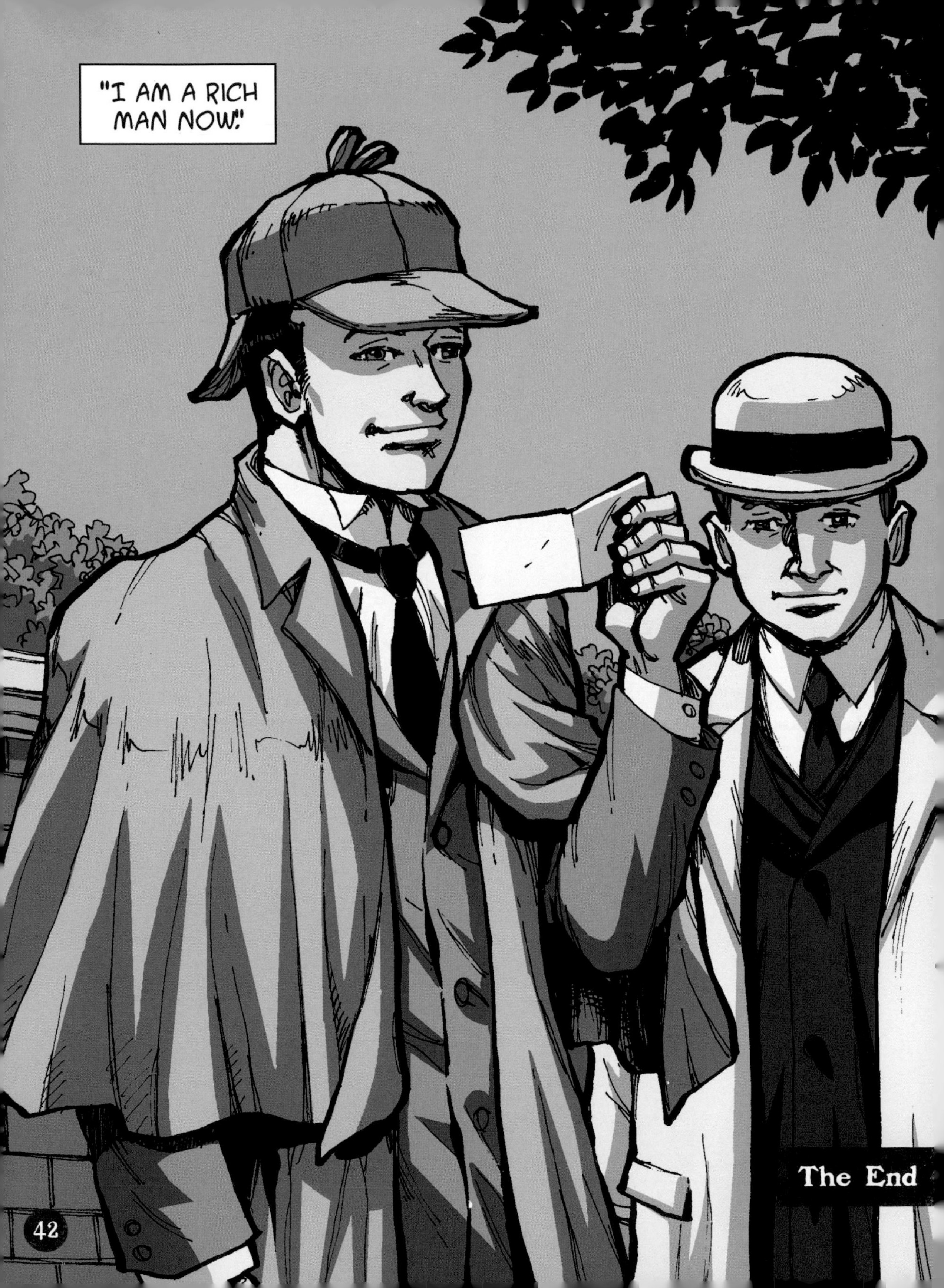
"I AM A RICH MAN NOW."
The End

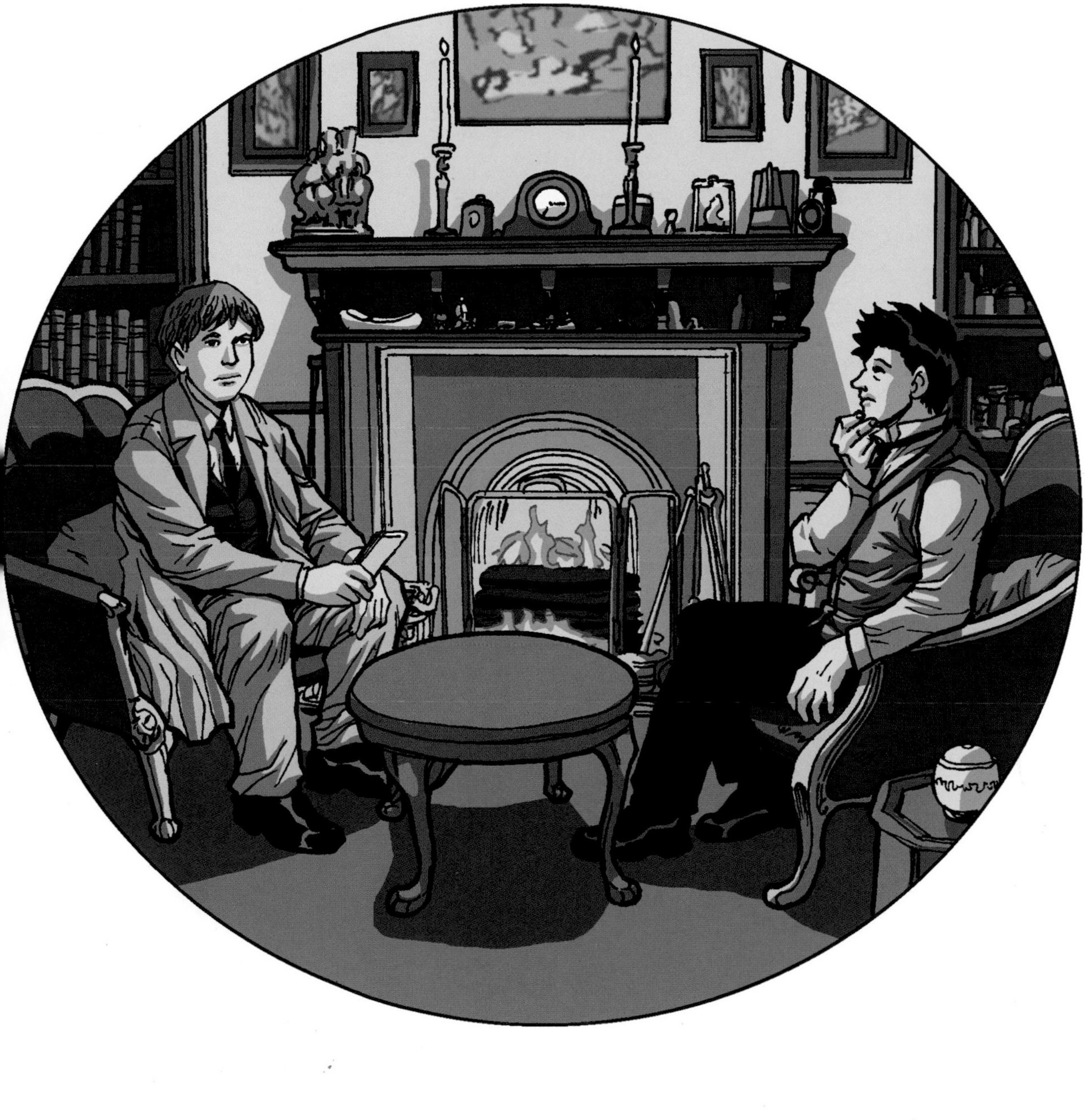

How to Draw Dr. John Watson

by Ben Dunn

Step 1: Use a pencil to draw a simple framework. You can start with a stick figure! Then add circles, ovals, and cylinders to get the basic form. Getting the simple shapes in place is the beginning to solving any great case.

Step 2: Time to add to Watson's look. Use the shapes you started with to fill in his clothes. Use guidelines to add circles for the eyes. And don't forget to make sure the hat covers the head, not floats on top of it.

Step 3: Now you can go in with a pen and start inking Watson. Fill in all the details and fix any mistakes. Let the ink dry to avoid smudges, then erase any pencil marks. Watson is ready for some color, so grab your markers and get started!

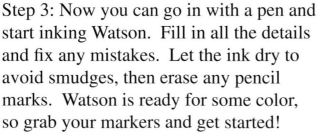

44

Glossary

alibi - a witness or evidence that proves someone was not present at a crime.

blackmail - to make threats to tell people of a crime unless the criminal does something for the blackmailer.

disposal - the power to make use of as one chooses.

enroll - to register, especially in order to attend a school.

felony - a serious crime that requires a heavy punishment.

handicap - a disadvantage that makes something difficult to accomplish.

homesickness - longing for home or family when away from them.

obvious - easily seen or understood; clear.

preparatory school - a private school to prepare students for a college or university education.

pursue - to follow someone or something.

ransom - money demanded for the release of a captive.

ruffian - a bully.

savage - wild and unkind. A member of a group of people who are not thought to be civilized.

select - of special value or excellence.

Web Sites

To learn more about Sir Arthur Conan Doyle, visit ABDO Group online. Web sites about Doyle are featured on our Book Links page. These links are routinely monitored and updated to provide the most current information available. **www. abdopublishing.com**

About the Author

Arthur Conan Doyle was born on May 22, 1859, in Edinburgh, Scotland. He was the second of Charles Altamont and Mary Foley Doyle's ten children. In 1868, Doyle began his schooling in England. Eight years later, he returned to Scotland.

Upon his return, Doyle entered the University of Edinburgh's medical school, where he became a doctor in 1885. That year, he married Louisa Hawkins. Together they had two children.

While a medical student, Doyle was impressed when his professor observed the tiniest details of a patient's condition. Doyle later wrote stories where his most famous character, Sherlock Holmes, used this same technique to solve mysteries. Holmes first appeared in *A Study in Scarlet* in 1887 and was immediately popular.

Between 1887 and 1927, Doyle wrote 66 stories and 3 novels about Holmes. He also wrote other fiction and nonfiction novels throughout his life. In 1902, Doyle was knighted for his work in a field hospital in the South African War. Four years later, Louisa died. Doyle married Jean Leckie in 1907, and they had three children together.

Sir Arthur Conan Doyle died on July 7, 1930, in Sussex, England. Today, Doyle's famous character, Sherlock Holmes, is honored with societies around the world that pay tribute to the detective.

Additional Works

A Study in Scarlet (1887)

The Mystery of Cloomber (1889)

The Firm of Girdlestone (1890)

The White Company (1891)

The Adventures of Sherlock Holmes (1891-92)

The Memoirs of Sherlock Holmes (1892-93)

Round the Red Lamp (1894)

The Stark Munro Letters (1895)

The Great Boer War (1900)

The Hound of the Baskervilles (1901-02)

The Return of Sherlock Holmes (1903-04)

Through the Magic Door (1907)

The Crime of the Congo (1909)

The Coming of the Fairies (1922)

Memories and Adventures (1924)

The Case-Book of Sherlock Holmes (1921-1927)

About the Adapters

Author

Vincent Goodwin earned his BA in Drama and Communications from Trinity University in San Antonio. He is the writer of three plays as well as the cowriter of the comic book *Pirates vs. Ninjas II.* Goodwin is also an accomplished journalist, having won several awards for his work as a columnist and reporter.

Illustrator

Ben Dunn founded Antarctic Press, one of the largest comic companies in the United States. His works appear in Marvel and Image comics. He is best known for his series *Ninja High School* and *Warrior Nun Areala.*